'They *must* be found, Himmler!' thundered the Führer over the 'phone from his HQ in East Prussia. 'I make you personally reponsible for them. You know well they are the bravest of the brave. I will not have them abandoned, even if they are deep in enemy territory. SS Assault Regiment Wotan is worth a whole division to Germany. Find them, Himmler, *find them!*'

Also by Leo Kessler

LEO KESSLER

The Outcasts

Wotan 22

Futura

A Futura Book

First published in Great Britain in 1986 by
Century Hutchinson Ltd, London

This edition published in 1988 by
Futura Publications, a division of
Macdonald & Co (Publishers) Ltd
London & Sydney

ISBN 0 7088 3646 1

Reproduced, printed and bound in Great Britain by
Hazell Watson & Viney Limited
Member of BPCC plc
Aylesbury, Bucks

Futura Publications
A Division of
Macdonald & Co (Publishers) Ltd
Greater London House
Hampstead Road
London NW1 7QX
A member of Pergamon MCC Publishing Corporation plc

'O soldier, soldier, where now are your eyes
That once so much did see?
The vultures have plucked them from his face
Just over our company.'

Karl Shapiro, 1945.

A NOTE BY PROFESSOR WASHINGTON LEE III

Who, today, knows anything of 'Black Jack' Petersen's Fighting Coons? Where is there any account of what happened in those snowbound French mountains in the winter of 1944? How Colonel Petersen's poor black soldiers, tricked by the SS, were massacred by planes of their *own* air force, commanded by an American, who later became a four-star general? The various US Department of Defense's monumental accounts of the campaign in Europe in World War Two do not even record the existence of Petersen's battalion. Nor does a more popular history of the surprise German attack in Alsace that winter – Charles Whiting's *Operation Northwind* – make any reference to the unit.

Why? Because in those days in a strictly segregated US Army, we black soldiers simply did not exist. We were truly the 'invisible men' of American society. As I vividly remember one of our white instructors, a true 'Georgia cracker', telling us draftees back in the summer of '42, 'You black boys were meant to shovel shit! But some smart jerk-off in Washington thinks they can make fighting soldiers outa ya!' And he cackled and spat in the dust contemptuously, as if the possibility that a black man could ever become a fighting infantryman was out of this world. Well, in spite of the prejudice against us and the fact that no general seemed to want us when we finally did reach the front, we *did* turn out to be fighting men. Indeed, we fought the elite of the elite, SS Assault Regiment Wotan! And we would have whipped them, too, if fate had not played such a cruel trick on us.

Herr Leo Kessler merits the recognition due to him for having re-discovered the sad and tragic story of 'Black Jack' Petersen's Fighting Coons before it is forgotten for ever. Back in those bad days, the US Chiefs of Staff briefing their generals on how to handle black *American* soldiers could write:

'He (the negro) is careless, shiftless, irresponsible and secretive. He is immoral, untruthful and his sense of right-doing is relatively inferior.' What gall! Leo Kessler has now shown just how patently untrue that bigoted statement was.

So here is the true story, at last, of how the 'Fighting Coons' fought their only battle of World War Two. Eight hundred brave young black men, thrown into combat against *Obersturmbannführer* von Dodenburg's SS, from which only two were to return: a white Jewish captain of supposedly homosexual tendencies and a single black master-sergeant, who has relived that tragedy up there in the snowbound mountains every day that has dawned since. It is not a pretty story, but in those days there were few *pretty* stories.

Washington Lee, Ph.D.
College Park,
University of Maryland (ex-master
sergeant 600th US Infantry Battalion)
December, 1985.

BOOK ONE

Adolf Hitler Commands!

'Führer befiehlt, wir gehorchen!'*

Motto of the Armed SS, 1944.

* 'Führer command, we obey.'

CHAPTER 1

'*Die Front?*'

'*Jawohl, Hauptsturm,*' the bald-headed pilot with the cocky grin answered, as the Fiesler Storch zoomed in low over the broad expanse of the Rhine and immediately began to gain height.

Next to him *Hauptsturmführer* Thomas, all gleaming silver badges and elegantly tailored uniform, staff officer written all over him, craned his head forward. Below them the flat Alsatian plain whizzed by. But his gaze was fixed on the Vosges Mountains beyond, looming up like a grey cliff, their peaks already tipped with the first snow of the year. He frowned. They were up there somewhere. But where, in God's name? It was nearly a week now since they had last contacted SS Headquarters, and *Reichsführer SS* Himmler was worried about them, exceedingly worried. Even the Führer, as hard-pressed as he was, trying to fight the enemy on both the eastern and western frontiers of the embattled Reich, had inquired about the lost regiment.

'They *must* be found, Himmler!' he had thundered over the 'phone from his HQ in East Prussia. 'I make you personally responsible for them. You know well they are the bravest of the brave. I will not have them abandoned, even if they are deep in enemy territory. SS Assault Regiment Wotan is worth a whole division to Germany. Find them, Himmler, *find them*!'

'Flying shit!' The little pilot's cynical voice cut into the elegant staff officer's reverie. '*Flak* to you, *Hauptsturm.*'

Without taking his eyes off the ground below, the pilot placed a steel helmet on his bald head and then began stuffing what looked like a car hub-cap into the webbing of his parachute harness where it passed between his legs.

Thomas forgot his own problems and asked, 'What's that for, *Oberfeldwebel?*'

The pilot gripped the controls in both hands as the first shell exploded in the air to their front, sending white-hot, steel scything lethally through the sky. 'Insurance, *Hauptsturm*!' he hissed through gritted teeth.

'Insurance?' Thomas gasped as, with a mighty crimson crash, a shell exploded to port, the shock buffeting the little monoplane like a blow from a gigantic fist.

The pilot forced a grin. 'I don't mind croaking it, sir, but I'd hate to have my tail shot off. The thought of not being able to dip my wick in that juicy honey-pot . . .' At that moment shells burst on either side of the little plane, filling the cabin with acrid cordite fumes and sending the Fiesler up fifty metres.

Thomas gasped and clutched at the nearest stanchion, his hands wet with the hot sweat of fear. '*Himmelherrgott*!' he cursed, licking lips which were suddenly parched. 'That was close!'

Down below the plain was alive with vicious bursts of fire as the enemy flak concentrated on the lone intruder.

'Old trick,' the pilot said. 'They're trying to bracket us. But the arses-with-ears have to get up earlier than this to cook my goose. Grab hold of your hat, *Hauptsturm*. Here we – GO!'

Abruptly he thrust the controls forward and the little plane was suddenly falling out of the sky at a tremendous rate. Thomas opened his mouth, ears popping madly. He tried to scream but couldn't. His stomach flipped. He felt himself pressed against the back of his seat as if a giant fist had slammed him against it. Nearer and nearer came the ground. Now, with eyes that bulged from his contorted, sweat-glazed face, he could see in every detail the white-baked roads, the patches of half-timbered farmhouses, the tiny groups of khaki-clad figures running for cover, a man frantically trying to set up a machine gun on a flat roof. *Would the pilot never level out? Was the damned Luftwaffe fool taking him to his death?*

'Arseholes up. Three cheers for America!' the sweating pilot roared suddenly. With a grunt he tugged at the controls. In the very last moment, when it seemed the little plane must shatter to pieces on the ground, it levelled out.

For a moment Thomas thought he would black out. He couldn't breathe and red and white stars were exploding in front of his bulging eyes. Then they were skimming across the surface of a lake, the flak behind them. Thomas breathed a sigh of relief and, with a hand that shook visibly, he wiped the beads of sweat from his forehead.

Next to him the pilot laughed. 'A real piss strainer, eh, *Hauptsturm*? I thought I was gonna buy the shitting farm just then. Now, what about a bit of map-reading for me, sir?' He nodded towards the west where the vanishing sun was tinging the peaks of the Vosges a blood-red hue.

'Light won't last much longer,' he said. 'I'd like to land this crate while I can still see.'

Thomas, recovered a little from the headlong dive, nodded his understanding. '*Verstanden*,' he snapped in that harsh efficient manner that all SS officers affected, and bent his head over the map spread out across his knees. The Fiesler flew on.

'*Thomas*!' Himmler had snapped, as outside in shattered Berlin the sirens began to sound the 'all clear' at last, 'it is of the utmost urgency that you find Colonel von Dodenburg and his men.'

'Sir!' Thomas had barked, feigning an eagerness which he did not feel. Berlin was bad enough this autumn of 1944, but still Number Ten Prinz Albrechtstrasse* possessed an exceedingly fine air-raid shelter and the little blonde typist in Himmler's outer office had an even better personal 'air-raid shelter', in which he had been burying himself very pleasantly these last few nights. It would be a crying shame to have to abandon all that for the dubious honour of trying to find the celebrated Colonel von Dodenburg.

'There will, of course, be a piece of tin in it for you – good

* Himmler's HQ

tin*,' Himmler had continued, 'if you find Wotan. That goes without saying.'

'Thank you, sir! Very good of you, sir!' Thomas had risen to the bait, as he knew was expected of him. *Reichsführer SS* Himmler believed that the whole world was only too eager to put their necks on the block in order to win a piece of cheap enamel to pin on their chests. Unconsciously Himmler tapped his own skinny, black-uniformed chest, as if to remind himself that his own 'Sport's Medal in Bronze', his sole decoration, was still in place.

Thomas waited. Outside, in the smoking rubble of the courtyard, someone was shouting in a tough, coarse Berlin voice, 'Pick her shitting head up and put it in the bucket, man! *Los . . . los . . .* It won't frigging well bite you. She ain't got no teeth, as it is. Ha ha!' Thomas swallowed hard and fought to repress a shudder at the thought of the severed head of some bomb victim being placed in a pail.

'Now then.' Himmler tapped the map spread out in front of him, eyes narrowing behind the schoolmaster's pince-nez he affected. 'The Americans reported that what was left of SS Wotan was destroyed – *here* – at the crossing of the River Isère after the evacuation of Montélimar.'**

Thomas nodded. He, personally, had removed the Regiment from the SS's Order-of-Battle after receiving that enemy report.

'However, Thomas, we know that was not the case. Old hare that he is, Colonel von Dodenburg somehow deluded the Amis and managed to smuggle what was left of his unit through their lines until he reached the neighbourhood of the Col de la Schluck, the pass into the Alsatian Plain – *here*. That was the last and only radio contact we have had with Colonel von Dodenburg.'

Himmler frowned, and sucked his teeth, as if he might be searching for a bad tooth.

---

* Slang for medals and decorations
** See '*March or Die*' for further details

Outside that tough Berlin voice was sneering, 'What kind of creeping Jesus are you man? What does a bit o' gore and brain matter? Yer can wash yer pinkies afterwards, you great big piss-pansy, you!'

'It's obvious, Thomas,' Himmler continued, ignoring the unknown rescue worker's crudities, 'that von Dodenburg found it impossible to break through the Franco-American ring around Colmar, which is held by what is left of our 19th Army. So what is he attempting to do?'

He had answered his own question. 'My guess he has taken to the Vosges – *here*. Somewhere to the east of Épinal, between Patton's Americans coming up from the west and the American Seventh Army coming up from the south. It would be the obvious thing for him to do. There is one real problem, however.'

'The terrain, sir?' Thomas judged it was time to say something.

'Exactly! In the condition von Dodenberg's men must be, the Vosges will present an almost impassable barrier for them. The first snow has already fallen and it won't be long before it starts to snow in earnest.' Himmler raised one well-manicured finger, almost, Thomas could not help thinking, like some child with a weak bladder asking to be excused in class. 'There is one way in which they can do it – the Crest Route.'

'*The Crest Route, Reichsführer?*' Thomas echoed in bewilderment, noting that, for the first time since he had entered Himmler's office, his sallow face had cracked into a wintry smile. *Reichsführer SS* Heinrich Himmler was suddenly very pleased with himself.

'I think now,' the pilot was saying, as the mountains grew ever closer, 'I can remove the old ballrace protector. My outside plumbing looks as if it's going to be safe for another day at least.' He grunted and tugged the hubcap from between his legs. 'Keep it there too long and yer tail gets damned sore.'

THE WOTAN ESCAPE ROUTE, SEPT 1944

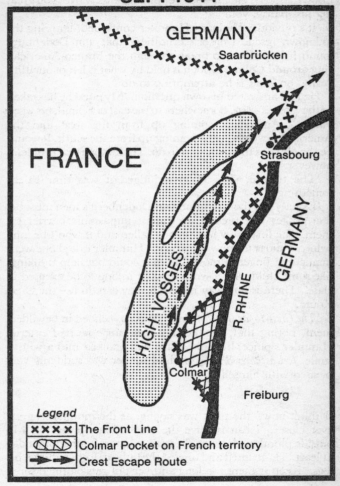

GERMANY

Saarbrücken

FRANCE

Strasbourg

HIGH VOSGES

R. RHINE

GERMANY

Colmar

Freiburg

Legend

xxxx	The Front Line
◯◯◯	Colmar Pocket on French territory
→→→	Crest Escape Route

'Will you be quiet about your stupid parts.' Thomas cut him off harshly, looking up from the map. 'According to my calculations we should be outside the enemy ring around the Colmar Pocket. I think we can start to come down now and begin looking for them.'

The pilot nodded his agreement, very business-like now. 'We'll work the grids, sir, if you agree. We'll cover each one in turn before moving on, heading on a basically northern course.'

'*Einverstanden*,' Thomas snapped. 'But can't you slow the plane up? The terrain down there is very rugged.' He stared down at the steep furrowed surface of the Vosges, covered here and there with great tracts of dark green firs marching up and down the slopes like columns of spike-helmeted Prussian guardsmen.

Dutifully the pilot throttled back, while Thomas began searching the ground below with his binoculars. The missing Wotan men, he told himself, might well have gone to ground on the higher slopes. There they could have found some German sympathizers, for the whole of Alsace was German-speaking. But on the plain the peasants waved with the wind. When the French were the bosses, they were pro-French; when the Germans were in control, they were pro-German. Up in the mountains, however, the peasants stuck to their old German traditions; they would remain loyal whoever it was that controlled Alsace. Systematically he surveyed each lonely, half-timbered farmhouse, while the pilot flew up and down the grids on the map.

Time passed and the pilot started to look more frequently at his fuel gauge, knowing that he needed at least ten minutes fuel in reserve to get him back across the Rhine and into the Reich. Below, the terrain had become even more rugged and there were fewer farmhouses. The roads, too, had given way to tracks, some of them patched with new snow. 'Arsehole of the world,' he commented sourly. 'Jesus H! What a dump!'

Thomas nodded and lowered his binoculars for a moment. 'I'm inclined to agree. Phew, they could be anywhere down

there! Those mountains could swallow up a whole division –
and we're looking for a mere handful, perhaps a couple of
hundred at the most.' He broke off suddenly; the pilot wasn't
listening.

'What is it?' he hissed, suddenly alarmed.

'Down there – at three o'clock. Can you see it. That hut!'

Thomas flashed up his binoculars. A small half-timbered
cottage, the beams blackened with age, slid into the twin
circles of calibrated glass. 'Yes?' he demanded.

'That cart – can you see it? Outside.'

'Yes, I see it. What about it?'

'That's no farmer's cart, *Hauptsturm*. Look at the colour
and the rubber wheels. That's a *Wehrmacht* hand-cart, the kind
the hairy-assed stubble-hoppers use to tow around their
machine guns, ammo and the like.'

'God in heaven, you're right,' Thomas exclaimed, rapidly
adjusting his binoculars. 'Do you think that it could be them?'

'We'll soon find out. Let's give them a buzz.' He pushed
forward the controls and the little Fiesler Storch started to
hurtle towards the ground once more.

Half a kilometre away on the opposite hillside, Colonel von
Dodenburg, staring through his binoculars at the diving
plane, groaned. '*Grosse Scheisse!*' he cursed. 'The first contact
we've had with our own people for over a week – *and now
they're heading straight for the trap*!'

CHAPTER 2

A tank lay on its side in the road; ripe apples from the orchard showered down all about. One of the crew, his uniform shredded by the explosion of the mine so that he was virtually naked, hung from one of the apple trees like some monstrous human fruit, the wrecked Mark III's gun thrust through his belly and protruding blood-red from his arched back.

Further on, there was the rest of the crew: an officer hit by one of the exploding shells, burst apart like an over-ripe marrow; a kid, perhaps sixteen, his teeth bared in the last frenzy of death, his clenched fist trying to stuff back his guts into the black-red hole of his ruined stomach; next to him a gunner, his upper body stripped to the rib-cage by the explosion, his bones gleaming like polished ivory in the September sunshine. And everywhere the flies, fat and greedy, feasting on the dead; while above the crows circled, waiting their turn to pick out the dead men's eyes.

Exhausted as they were, they had been appalled at the sight, as they filtered warily out of the trees and down to the mountain road, staggering to a ragged halt. Only Schulze had reacted. Angrily he had raised his Schmeisser and fired a burst at the birds above, crying, 'Fart off, you frigging greedy shitehawks! Fart off!'

His angry cry had seemed to rouse the others from their shocked lethargy. Colonel von Dodenburg, his handsome face covered in dust, his uniform almost in rags, gasped, 'Sentries out. Form a perimeter, men. *Los, los.*'

Next to him one-legged Corporal Matz had taken up the cry, snarling, '*Los, los,* you bunch of cardboard soldiers. Get the lead outa yer skinny, soft asses!'

Staggering as if they were drunk, the young soldiers, who had survived the débâcle of Montélimar and the long march north, fell to their knees in the trees, weapons raised, while the tall blond Colonel advanced warily on the wrecked tank. Behind him Matz and Schulze, the old running mates, followed, eyes cautious, fingers cocked around the triggers of their automatics.

'What do you think, sir?' Shulze whispered hoarsely, awed now by the terrible spectacle. 'Who croaked them?'

Von Dodenburg, crouched slightly, continued advancing, not taking his eyes off the ruined tank for one instant. 'Mine by the looks of it. Can you see that scorched part of the road? Planted there, I suspect.'

'By who, sir?' Schulze asked.

Von Dodenburg shrugged. 'Can't be the Americans or the French. We haven't seen any of them for two days now. They haven't reached this part of the world yet.'

'Frigging frog partisans then, sir? That kind of murderous bastard, sniping our lads from behind . . .'

Suddenly the machine gun positioned in the trees to the right of the mountain road burst into action, slugs racing up the cobbles towards the three SS men, striking them in angry spurts of blue flame.

'*Hit the dirt*!' von Dodenburg cried and fell to the ground as a second burst ran the length of the wrecked tank and thudded into the naked body perched in the tree. As if in slow motion, animated by the slugs, it started to free itself from the branches and slip to the ground like some ghastly corpse raised from the dead. But the weary troopers of SS Assault Regiment Wotan had no time or eyes for the dead tanker. Already they were beginning to snap off single shots at their unseen assailants in the woods to their front, even the youngest keenly aware that they could not afford to waste ammunition.

Von Dodenburg knew it too. He had no intention of fighting a pitched battle on this lonely road, while the partisans, if that was what they were, brought up reinforcements and trapped them for good. 'Listen to me, you troopers,' he yelled above the angry snap-and-crackle of small-arms fire. 'We're going to break off this action. We three will throw grenades. As soon as the first one explodes and rattles them,' he said a silent prayer that his opponents would, indeed, be rattled, 'start pulling back into the trees. *Got it?*'

'*Got it, sir!*' half-a-dozen lusty young voices yelled back, and again von Dodenburg was glad that he had such men, youngsters as they were for the most part, under his command.

'Right then, get ready to move out!' Von Dodenburg waited no longer. He did not even look behind him at the two NCOs lying in the road; they were old hares. They didn't need any orders from him. He pulled the last remaining stick grenade from his shabby, battered boot, ripped off the pin and counted to four. On the count of four, he hurled the grenade at the wood to his right. It exploded in a flash of blinding white light. Someone screamed, high and hysterical like a woman in agony, and then von Dodenburg was on his feet, head bent as the shrapnel pattered down on his helmet. Behind him, as he started to back off, firing controlled bursts from the hip to left and right, Schulze and Matz threw their grenades as one. Abruptly the machine gun to the right stopped firing and what looked like an abandoned football, painted red, rolled slowly down the road towards them – *a human head!*

But the three of them did not have any time to dwell on the new horror. Running and firing, they backed off, as, to the rear, the Wotan troopers fled for the cover of the trees from which they had almost walked into the trap that had been set for them. Five minutes later von Dodenburg and the two noncoms had disappeared too. But even as he had done so, von Dodenburg had realized, with an abrupt sinking feeling, that they were in trouble, real trouble. Schulze had too, for he had shouted in the same instant that the first of their unknown assailants had slunk out in the open, weapons blazing as they began to follow the retreating Germans. '*Now the tick-tock really is in the frigging pisspot!*'

*

All the rest of that day and well into the following one, the men of Wotan had been chased through the wooded hills, stumbling, scared and exhausted, down the green forest trails, emaciated bodies tensed for the first startling burst of machine-gun fire which would indicate that their enemy had found them once again.

Von Dodenburg, desperately trying to find a way out of the trap before it was too late, guessed their pursuers were from some Southern French *maquis* band. More than once he had caught glimpses of their olive-skinned faces under shocks of jet-black hair, so unlike the stolid, Germanic-looking Alsatians of the neighbourhood. Obviously they had moved north behind the victorious Franco-Americans to loot and pillage the rich farmlands of France's eastern province, which, being annexed to the Reich for most of the war, had been favoured and spoiled by the German administration.

'Great crap on the Christmas tree!' he had cursed more than once to the hollow-eyed, bearded Schulze, 'can we *never* lose the obstinate bastards?' And to that overwhelming question not even 'Frau Schulze's handsome son', as he invariably called himself with a total lack of modesty, could find an answer.

Now, however, as the little Fiesler dived unsuspectingly towards that lone farmhouse with the *Wehrmacht* cart outside and from which a bunch of 'obstinate bastards' were presently holding up Wotan, it came to von Dodenburg with the total, one hundred per cent, revelation of a vision.

'Schulze, you big-horned ox,' he snapped, not taking his eyes off the diving plane for an instant, 'what do you think would happen if the Fiesler crashed?'

Schulze looked at his C.O.'s hollow face, the lean cheeks lined with a sheen of golden stubble. 'You mean the frog arse-with-ears?'

'Yes.'

'They'd be out there, seeing what they could get their greedy little claws into. Pistols, cameras, imagine what they could get for any gas they could salvage from the wreck. It would be worth a small fortune on the frog black market!'

'Exactly,' von Dodenburg agreed, trying not to look at an anxious Matz, who was tensed with his Schmeiser raised, as if he were intending to fire a burst into the air at any moment to warn the pilot plunging to his death.

'What are you thinking, sir?' Schulze asked hastily, the roar of the plane's engine filling the whole sky now.

'This. If that plane crashes, they'll be off running for the wreck like a shot and . . .'

'*We'll be taken off the hook*!' Schulze yelled above the ear-splitting racket, eyes suddenly full of disbelief.

Von Dodenburg caught the look. 'It's the only way, Schulze!' he cried, as if attempting to convince himself. 'There are two hundred of us. Only two of them.' He looked miserably at Schulze. 'It's the only way, old house,' he added.

Next to them, Matz dropped his Schmeisser. The little plane hurtled down on its dive of death.

The first burst of fire shattered the cockpit. The perspex in front of the pilot had been transformed into a glittering spiderweb of broken crystals. Next to him the SS officer screamed. A series of red buttonholes, bubbling pink foam, appeared suddenly along the front of his tunic. '*Mutti, Mutti*!' he cried pathetically, his agony turning him into a little child again. Dark-red blood started to trickle from his nostrils. His head slumped down on his ruined chest. He was dying.

But the pilot had other things on his mind than the dying SS officer. Taking one boot off their flying rudder, he slammed it against the shattered perspex. It did the trick. The fragments showered outwards and he could see the dark figures scattering wildly below as he hurtled towards them in his dive of death. To the right a machine gun was still spitting tracer towards him, the white slugs racing upwards in a graceful curve, gathering speed by the second.

Frantically he wrenched at the controls as the engine began to splutter alarmingly. *Nothing happened!* The plane continued on its collision course. He levered one foot against the front of the cockpit, the cold wind making him blink with tears. His muscles thrust against the thin material of his flying jacket. His eyes bulged and the veins stood out like purple wires at his temples, as he exerted every last bit of strength.

Suddenly the plane's nose came up. He almost wet himself with relief. Stuttering and spluttering, the engine continued to fire, as the crippled plane swept a mere fifty metres above the roof of the farmhouse, trailing black smoke behind it, the angry maquis below peppering the sky with fire.

'Great balls of bullshit!' he cried, besides himself with relief. 'We've done it, *Hauptsturm*! *We've frigging well done it*!' He risked a quick glance at the young staff officer. But it was already too late. He lay slumped there, mouth gaping stupidly, eyes unseeing, his blood dripping steadily to the floor of the cockpit. *Hauptsturmbannführer* Thomas, who had delighted in that little blonde typist's 'personal air-raid shelter' would never visit that particularly pleasurable refuge again. He was dead.

Colonel von Dodenburg wasted no more time, as the plane, trailing thick black smoke, disappeared over the ridge, followed by the excited Maquis who had held the farmhouse. He pumped his clenched right fist up and down rapidly three times. It was the infantry signal for attack. His men did not hesitate. They, too, knew the importance of speed. It was vital that they broke out while the Maquis were distracted by the plane. They surged forward through the firs, lean ruthless faces animated by the need to kill and survive, eyes suddenly gleaming and fanatical once more, covered with a kind of crazy sheen like those of a madman.

A Maquis popped up from a bush to the right, swarthy face dwarfed by a floppy black beret. He raised his sub-machine gun but Schulze didn't give him a chance to fire it. He lashed out with his jackboot like some graceful Thai boxer. The boot connected with the Frenchman's chin. There was a horrible, nauseating click. The Frenchman shot back, his neck broken, blood jetting from his nose. They ran on blindly.

A grenade, spluttering and trailing smoke, came hurtling out of the trees. Von Dodenburg grabbed it even before it hit the ground. The next instant he had thrown it back the way it had come. There was a blinding flash, a yell of pain and the Maquis who had thrown it came tumbling out of the trees in a shower of green. Matz thrust home his bayonet into the Frenchman's quivering body without even stopping running.

Up front, Schulze chortled, 'That's the stuff to give the troops, Matzi! Not bad for a half-cripple!'

'Another word from you, Schulzi,' Matz gasped, doing his best to keep up with the others, 'an' I'll shove me pegleg up yer ass!'

'Ooh!' Schulze quavered in a mock falsetto, 'kiss me quick, *Schatzi*! I think I've just fallen in love with you!'

Matz cursed and von Dodenburg shook his head in mock wonder. They ran on.

The little pilot, face glazed with sweat, as if greased with vaseline, knew it was now or never. The Feisler was shaking frighteningly, as if it might fall apart at any moment. The motor was giving off strange choking sobs. He freed a hand for an instant and wiped the sweat from his forehead. Down below the firs whizzed by like a dark green carpet, broken here and there by craggy grey outcrops of rock, bare of vegetation. He swallowed. The Fiesler could land on a tea-towel, or so its pilots boasted. But this one was going to be a piss-strainer, a real balls-breaker. How in three devils' name was he going to land successfully on one of those uphill slopes?

'Well, if you don't, old house,' a cynical little voice inside him answered, 'they'll be using what's left of you to make meatballs.' The engine gave one last anguished sob and died with an awesome, mechanical death-rattle.

Now there was no sound save for the hiss of the wind through the shattered cockpit. The plane started to come

down rapidly, the pines racing up to meet it. The pilot tensed.
This was it!

The port wing tipped the pines. Green shreds flew
everywhere. In the very last moment, his nerves ticking
electrically, his body soaked and lathered with sweat, he
managed to right the crippled plane. To his front a clearing in
the forest. A stretch of a hundred metres or so of naked rock,
littered with huge boulders. 'Holy strawsack!' he gasped and
gripped the controls in hands that were white at the knuckles.
There was a ripping sound. He felt a burst of icy air at his feet.
Something had torn away the crate's guts. Now the ground
was racing up to meet him at an alarming rate. Desperately
he forced up the Fiesler's nose a little. It did the trick. The
plane was effectively braked. Eyes narrowed to slits, he
tensed. The Fiesler hit the ground. Almost immediately it
bounced up again like a rubber ball. A moment later it
slammed down once more in a great grinding roar. The
undercarriage collapsed.

At one hundred kilometres an hour, the crippled plane
raced across the rocks, trailing a huge wake of pebbles and
dust behind it. A huge boulder loomed. He flung the controls
to one side. Somehow it worked. The Fiesler slid by the rock.
A wing snapped and fell off like a metallic leaf. Still, the plane
did not overturn. A tree came hurtling into view. Beyond lay
a tremendous drop to the valley below. This had to be it!

The sweating pilot, his strength almost exhausted, his
shoulders and arms afire with the ordeal of holding on to this
crazy piece of aerial wreckage, aimed the Fiesler at it. It stood
in exactly the right place to act as a brake. If it failed,
then. . . . He dare not think that particularly horrible
thought to its ultimate end. Suddenly he found himself
praying as he had never prayed before. The drop came ever
closer. He was petrified with fear. *He was not going to make it!*

He let go of the controls. Sobbing with fear, he closed his
eyes and let it happen. He was going to go over the side of the
mountain. . . .

CHAPTER 3

'Sodomy is specifically denounced as an offence under the provisions of the 93rd Article of War. Administrative discharge is *not* the answer!' the harsh, authoritarian voice echoed up and down the corridors of Seventh Army's HQ at Vittel. 'War Department's policy, reflecting the express intention of Congress, is that *all* cases of sodomy should be court-martialled.'

'But sir,' another voice, a little angry, a little sad, was saying, 'the guy's got three Purple Hearts and he's been in combat since Sicily. Some of those dogfaces in the line don't see a dame for months on end. Most of them are bomb-happy, as it is. Can't we put it down to combat fatigue and . . .'

'Sodomy cases must be court-martialled and that's my final word on the subject. Do you read me?'

'Yes, sir, I read you,' the other man answered sadly. 'I'll start processing charges against the poor bastard immediately.'

Captain Wolf gave one of those cunning, lop-sided grins of his and shook his head, reminding himself that he was back in the world of the Top Brass. The guys who were the furthest from the firing line were always the keenest for action.

A group of clerks, male and female, came down the corridor to meet him. One of the men stared at the little man's rumpled uniform and tarnished silver bars, then gave a reluctant salute. One of the female WACs giggled. Wolf smiled softly. He knew he didn't look the part of an officer one bit, nor did he live up to his name or profession, which was that of a spy-master. He was small and undersized, already bent-shouldered like some cloistered academic, and the general picture of shabby harmlessness was complemented by his prominent buck teeth and the thick, horn-rimmed glasses he was forced to wear. As his boss, Chief of Seventh Army Intelligence, Briga-dier-General Peters, had commented sourly more than once, '*Wolf? You look more like a goddam jack-rabbit to me, Captain!*'

But the hot-tempered Brigadier-General knew that the awkward-looking and academic Wolf, with his gentle, almost feminine manner, was the Seventh Army's best Intelligence operative. Hadn't he discovered the wop spy who was signalling the location of US troops to that feared Kraut cannon 'Anzio Annie' on bloody Anzio beach back in Italy? Hadn't Wolf been the guy who had winkled out the enemy 'sleeper' network of agents, which they left behind after they had evacuated Rome? And the little New York Jew, whom he half-suspected of being a 'fruit', had very definitely been the only Intelligence operative under his command to work out the complexities of the French Resistance movement; and that the commie groups were *not* working for Charley de Gaulle, but for the goddam Russians in Moscow!

Now, as Wolf knocked hesitantly on his door and then entered, General Peters swung his cowboy boots off his desk, jerked the big cigar to the corner of his mouth, and cried exuberantly, 'Where in Sam Hill have you been, Wolf? You look as if you've just been thrown out of a goddam gin mill!'

The big, bluff Intelligence General, who affected a couple of ivory-handled revolvers in the style of his hero Patton, didn't wait for an answer. Instead he boomed, 'All right, take a weight off'n ya feet.' He pushed a bottle of *Bushmills* towards Wolf, together with a glass, and commanded, 'Okay, don't stand there like a spare penis at a wedding. Give yerself a snort, man!' Wolf poured himself a small drink of the bourbon, under the Brigadier's critical gaze, and took a delicate sip. Peters shook his head in mock disgust and then barked, 'All right, Wolf, when's the shit gonna hit the fan? Whatya hear?'

Wolf cleared his throat carefully and looked over the tops of his glasses at the General, who was levelling his cigar at him like a deadly weapon. 'The situation is . . . somewhat complicated, sir,' he began hesitantly.

'Then make it uncomplicated. *Shoot!*'

'I think,' again Wolf chose his words with care, almost as if he were thinking them out as he spoke, 'that Higher

Headquarters is being too complacent. The general mood is that we've got the Krauts licked in Europe. It's only a matter of weeks now before they surrender. Bring the boys home for Christmas sort of thing, sir.'

Peters nodded, his big bluff face looking a little worried now. 'Yes, I think I'll agree with you there, Wolf. That chase across France was too goddam easy. Now the Krauts are gonna fight on their own ground and from my experience – and I've fought 'em in two wars – they're not about to give up so easy.'

'I would say a little more, sir,' Wolf said in that careful manner of his.

'How do you mean?' Peters glowered at him and took a puff at his cigar.

'They might well be tempted to go over to the offensive and catch us with our pants down.'

'*Offensive!*' Peters exclaimed, sitting bolt upright in his chair. 'Are you out of your mind, man? Hell, we've just run 'em half across Europe! Fight they will over there on the Rhine, I am sure, but offensive!' He gasped for breath. 'Why, that's completely out of the question!' His jowls wobbled with the effort of so much speaking and flushed red. He reached out for the bottle of Bourbon and poured himself a hefty swig.

Wolf took his time, completely unmoved by the General's outburst, or so it seemed. Outside, in another office, the voice of the major he had heard when he had first entered the Headquarters was saying in a dry, bored sort of a way, 'Okay, Lee, now type this into your machine . . . buggery, contrary to the 93rd Article of War, First Lieutenant Horace Greeley Hawkins is charged that on 5th September, 1944, in a foxhole of the said company, wilfully and knowingly, and with indecent, lewd and lascivious intent did attempt to insert the penis of him, the said. . . .'

Wolf flushed and lowered his eyes modestly and Peters told himself his judgement was correct; the little kike was a fruit. To cover his own and Wolf's embarrassment, he snapped, 'All right, out with it. Let me hear your reasoning.'

'Well, sir, first we have a sizeable number of Germans –
some one hundred thousand of them still on our side of the
Rhine . . .'

'The German Pocket around Colmar below Strasbourg?'

'Yes sir, and in direct contact along the Rhine with the
Reich. An ideal spot for launching an offensive against us – a
base right in the middle of two Allied armies.'

Peters nodded. 'Agreed, but at the moment they are just
holding on. Not making any warlike signs at all.'

'Yes sir. The warlike signs are coming from within the
Reich. Speer* is making a terrific attempt to re-arm the
German divisions in the West. They're calling up seventeen-
year-olds by the thousand to fill up the gaps in their ranks.
But more importantly for me, sir, in counter-intelligence,
they're making contacts again at night with their sleepers all
along the borders with the Reich, from here in Alsace, right
through Lorraine, into Luxembourg and Belgium, way up to
Holland. At night you can hear the Kraut morse buzzing out
messages to their agents over here all the time, night after
night. So why are they contacting them if they are not
intending to use them in some sort of coming offensive?'

'Point taken, Wolf. But perhaps they are only trying to find
out our dispositions for the coming attack into the Reich from
them? Have you ever thought that that was the reason?'

'Yes, I have, sir. But we know that at the present time our
own Seventh Army is in no position to attack because of the
Krauts in the Colmar Pocket. We are simply marking time,
containing them. Why, then, contact agents in Alsace? But
there is something else, sir,' Wolf continued hastily, not
allowing Peters to interrupt. 'This was found yesterday by
one of my commie agents. He is working with some of those
Maquis from the south who are terrorizing the local farmers.'
Wolf dug inside his tunic and brought out a dirty piece of rag,
stained a dark russet colour, almost, Peters couldn't help
thinking, that of dried blood. Carefully Wolf placed the

---

* Minister of Armaments

object on the table next to the Bourbon, glanced at the General and then, after an instant, began to unfurl the cloth to reveal what the little parcel contained. Peters gasped, opened his mouth to say something, thought better of it, took a swift pull at his whisky and stared at the object, gaping like some surprised village yokel.

'To sum up,' the voice in the next office broke the horrified silence as the two Intelligence officers continued to stare at the ghastly object before them, 'this officer has been caught in *flagrante delicto*, committing sodomy on the body of Private First Class F.G. Sanders, Junior, of the United States Army, then being in a state of war. That's it,' he said with an air of finality. 'I only hope the poor bastard's smart enough to commit suicide while he's still in the Queer Stockade.'

'What in Sam Hill *is* it?' Peters gasped at last, tearing his gaze away from the charred, shrunken paw, protruding from the singed sleeve with the fire-faded legend above, '*Leibstandarte Adolf Hitler*'. He gulped hard, head twisted to one side, his face suddenly purple and hectic like a man being strangled.

'According to the dog tag that goes with it, also supplied by my obliging little frog, the owner of that bit of charred meat was one *Haupsturmbannführer* Helmut Thomas, who, I have discovered from my list of SS officers is – excuse, me, sir, *was* – second adjutant to *Reichsführer SS* Heinrich Himmler.'

General Peters was suitably impressed. 'You mean the big shot himself?'

'Exactly, sir.'

'So what's the adjutant of Himmler doing flying over Alsace, Wolf?' Peters asked, his complete bewilderment all too obvious.

'My informant tells me that there are SS up in the high Vosges. His outfit had been chasing them for forty-eight hours before they lost them when the plane crashed, carrying what's left of our friend there. Put two and two together and we come up with this – the late, unlamented Helmut was trying to contact those SS men.' He stopped and stared challengingly at his boss.

General Peters said nothing. He sat slumped there, his brow wrinkled; a brooding silence fell over the office, broken only by the clatter of typewriters and the ringing of telephones elsewhere.

Wolf saw that, tough as he was, Peters was a worried man. If the US Seventh Army was caught by surprise by the Krauts the finger would be laid upon him. As Chief of Intelligence it was his responsibility to see that the Seventh was always prepared for the enemy's next move. All the same, Peters did not dare cry wolf too often; most senior staff officers were sceptical of Intelligence's apparently constant gloom. In short, Wolf told himself, at this moment Peters was a man with his dong in the wringer!

'Let me go over the ground again, Wolf,' Peters broke the silence. 'According to your information, one, the Krauts are alerting their agents in the Alsace area?'

Wolf nodded.

'Two, we've got a bunch of SS men wandering around up in the High Vosges to no good purpose?'

Again Wolf nodded.

'Three, top-level SS Headquarters has tried to get in touch with those Krauts – for what reason we do not know?'

'Yes sir.'

'O.K. Wolf, let's get on the stick. Let's try to find out what those SS jerks are doing up there,' Peters snapped, suddenly irritated, for reasons known only to himself. He jabbed the big cigar towards the other man threateningly. 'I wanna know what game those SS men are playing, and I wanna know *fast*!'

'But, sir, it's not going to be so easy as that,' Wolf protested. 'As you know, Seventh Army is stretched to the utmost. We're holding the Rhine front from the Swiss frontier to the Saar. Where are we going to find the troops to tackle those SS men up there in the mountains? The barrel's pretty well scraped bare, sir.'

Peters grinned at him, but there was no warmth in the smile. Indeed, Wolf, on later reflection, would characterize it as positively malicious. 'Troops,' he said, 'you want troops? Why, hell, Wolf, I've got a whole goddam battalion, eight hundred strong, for you, if you're prepared to take them into the Vosges to find these SS Heinies!'

'A whole battalion!' Wolf echoed incredulously.

'Yep. Black Jack Petersen's Battalion's been hanging around these headquarters too long, or so he tells me. They're getting fat and sassy from too much good living . . .'

'But, sir,' Wolf interrupted, too shocked to be concerned with military protocol, 'Colonel Petersen's Battalion is coloured, sir.'

'Yep, you've got it in one, Wolf. I'm giving you *Petersen's coons!*'

'Black men to fight the cream of the SS . . .' Wolf began to protest, but Brigadier-General Peters drowned his objection in a great burst of laughter, as if he had just cracked a tremendous joke. '*Petersen's coons,*' he chortled, hugely amused. 'That's what you're getting – *Petersen's coons!*'

Five minutes later Captain Wolf was walking down the corridor in a daze as he considered his new mission with 'Petersen's coons'.

'And what will they do with him, Major?' the unseen enlisted man from the Judge Advocate's branch was asking.

'Do with him?' the Major answered. 'If the colonel has his way they'll hang, draw and quarter him, and then some.' He sighed like a sorely troubled man. 'But I guess in the end they'll just sentence him to life at Leavenworth.'

At that moment even that grim prospect seemed decidedly more attractive to the little counter-intelligence man than that of taking a battalion of blacks into the mountains to find and fight the SS.

Captain Wolf stepped out into the thin September sunshine and signalled for his driver. A minute later he was on his way to the barracks outside Vittel to find 'Petersen's coons'. The mission had commenced.

CHAPTER 4

Pains stabbed up and down his injured arm. His head seemed to be opening and shutting to the steady beat of a kettle-drum, but the icy wind blowing from the snowy mountain peaks was soothing his battered head and he felt alive and defiant for the first time since the crash. For a few minutes he crouched there in the pines, the briefcase he had taken from the dead SS officer clutched to his chest, as if it were very precious. Which in a way it was, that is, if he could find the elusive SS men of the missing regiment who were up there somewhere. He had reasoned from the start, ever since he had crawled away from the wreckage of the smashed plane and made his escape, that his salvation lay with the Wotan troopers. If he could find them he would be safe; but he knew the SS. Hard bastards they were, who would not take kindly to unnecessary ballast such as an injured *Luftwaffe* pilot, who was useless with a firearm. He had to offer them something and that something was the papers the SS officer had been carrying. Bring them the papers that the dead man had been ordered to deliver to them and they'd take care of him, he was sure. He forced himself to move on again, heading for the thin wisp of grey smoke trailing lazily into the sky above the next line of green pines. He had spotted it half an hour before and had been heading towards it ever since, hoping, perhaps irrationally, that whoever was there tending the fire would somehow lead him to the SS.

Now he broke through the scrub, nostrils sensing the wood smoke, tensed for the first angry shout, the bark of a dog, the crack of a rifle. Nothing happened. He turned a bend in the trail. There it was. A dismal, forbidding stone-and-wood cottage, withered yellow tobacco leaves hanging from the eaves, a great pile of maize to the right of the door for the animals, wherever they might be – but no sign of a human being.

He transferred the briefcase to his left hand and drew his pistol. Cautiously, very cautiously, hardly making a sound on the cobbled path which led to the door, he advanced towards it, a nerve at the side of his haggard unshaven face ticking electrically. Now he was only ten metres away. The smell of wood smoke was mixed with the usual farmyard odours of manure, boiled cabbage and sweat. The place was definitely lived in. The question was – by whom? Desperately he prayed that the occupants would be pro-German.

A creak. The pilot stopped dead, his heart missing a beat. The weathered, unpainted door was beginning to open slowly. He swallowed hard and gripped his pistol tighter. Then the wrinkled face of a very old woman appeared. She saw the pilot crouching there and tucked her face into her long scraggy neck like the dart of a snake's tongue. Frantically she tried to close the door, but he didn't give her a chance. He sprang at her, the adrenalin pumping new energy into his bloodstream. One hand shot out and he caught her by the scrawny throat. Next moment he pushed her forward with all his strength and she slammed against a bare wooden table, which seemed to be the miserable place's only furniture, whimpering like a spoiled child.

For a moment the two of them were locked together like exhausted lovers, while he glared fiercely at her terrified face, the tears trickling down her raddled cheeks. Then slowly he relaxed his grip, his pistol still pointed at her heart, until he released her altogether.

'Do you speak German?' he asked.

She swallowed hard as if her throat hurt and answered, 'Yes, I do,' in the thick guttural dialect of Alsace.

He breathed a sigh of relief and lowered his pistol. 'All right, granny, hurry it up. Get me some food.'

'Yes sir! At once, sir!' she answered dutifully and shuffled off to the wood stove in the corner, as if she were used to strangers like this coming into her home every day and ordering her about.

The pilot slumped gratefully onto one of the rough wooden

chairs and watched as she broke some eggs into a frying pan, licking his lips in anticipation as they began to sizzle and crackle in the hot fat. Suddenly he realized how hungry he was; he hadn't eaten for nearly two days now. 'God Almighty,' he told himself, 'I could eat a frigging horse.'

But he was not destined to enjoy his food. Just as the old crone placed the tin plate with the eggs and a lump of black bread in front of him, a tough North German voice barked, 'All right, soldier, get yersen and yer snout outa that trough and stand up – *careful like*! Put yer flippers in the air while yer doing so as well!'

The pilot started as if someone had thrust a red-hot needle into his back. The eggs forgotten immediately he started to rise to his feet, eyes fixed on the old crone's terrified face.

'Turn round!' the tough North German voice commanded. He turned and his heart skipped a beat with joy. An enormous man filled the doorway, Schmeisser held in his huge paw as if it were a child's toy; he wore the camouflaged tunic of the SS. 'Christ on a crutch!' the pilot gasped with relief, 'Am I ever glad to see you!'

'Hold yer piss!' the big man grunted, eyes narrowing greedily as he spotted the eggs. Without taking his gaze off the pilot and the eggs, he said to a little man behind him, 'Matzi, frisk him first and then get me them eggs. I ain't had an egg in ages.'

'What about me, Schulze?' the little man asked. 'What do I get?'

'My dice-beaker up yer slack ass, if yer don't move it!' Schulze grunted, licking his lips in anticipation. 'Rank hath its privileges, you little ape turd, and that includes eggies, all of 'em! Now move it!' Corporal Matz 'moved it', grumbling as he did so.

Matz, the old crone and the pilot watched fascinated as Schulze swallowed the eggs, one by one, the yolk staining his bearded chin, and giving a grunt of appreciation as yet another slipped into his gullet delightfully. When he was finished he belched pleasurably, then, seemingly as afterthought, he raised his right haunch, cried, 'Beware of green gas!' and gave one of his celebrated, extended musical farts. The old woman blanched, threw her apron over her face and fled into the corner.

'Insult to injury,' Matz mumbled grumpily. 'First you feed the buggers, then they fart at yer! There ain't no justice in this frigging world.' He wiped a dewdrop from the end of his beaky nose and flung it at the wall angrily.

'Knock it off plush-ears,' Schulze said, pleased with himself. 'Yer senior noncoms have got to have more nourishment than yer ordinary, common-or-garden stubble-hoppers, 'cos they use more brain power, see.' He tapped his forehead significantly with a finger like a hairy pork sausage.

'Brain power,' Matz grumbled, 'you've got a fat fart in your head, Schulze!'

The sergeant-major ignored his old running-mate. Instead he turned his attention to the *Luftwaffe* pilot. 'All right, fly-boy,' he boomed, 'let's hear it again, now that the inner pig-dog has been temporarily satisfied.' He rubbed his guts with pleasure to illustrate where the 'inner pig-dog' was located.

The pilot, happy to be with his own people again, even if they were the SS, told his story and explained how his passenger, bearing orders for Wotan, had been killed.

'So what were the orders?' Schulze asked.

'If they're in that case, it's locked and I haven't got the key,' the pilot answered, while the old crone continued to stare at them as if they were creatures from another world. 'All I know is that he told me you were going to take the Crest Route through the mountains.'

'And what's that when it's at home?' Matz asked.

The pilot shrugged. 'Search me. All I know is that if you're going to get out of this mess up here, you've got to find a route through the Vosges . . .' He stopped abruptly, the happy look vanishing from his face.

'What is it?' Schulze asked as he turned round, following the direction of the pilot's gaze.

Through the open door he could see tiny figures on the

horizon, well spread out and moving forward carefully, as if they were searching for something.

'Yours?' The pilot found his tongue again.

Schulze shook his head. 'No, our people are up in the woods a kilometre from here. They're frog partisans . . . and they're looking for us.'

Matz jerked up his Schmeisser. 'Come on then, Schulze, don't just stand there waiting for the fart to hit the side of the thunderbox. Let's get the shit out of here – *smartish*!'

'Yes, Sergeant-Major, we'd better be off,' the pilot agreed, grabbing the briefcase.

'Hold yer horses,' Schulze growled, his brow creased in thought. 'The Prussians don't shoot that quick! Listen, if we make a run for it and they spot us they'll follow us to where the lads are resting up and that lot of piss-pansies are in no fit state to start running again.' Schulze turned to the old woman and said, 'Start clearing the place up. Get rid of them plates and pan. And listen,' he hissed threateningly, grabbing the front of his trousers, 'if you let on to them that we've been here, *I'll stick my salami in so deep that yer glassy orbits'll pop right out*!'

She gasped and immediately started to bustle about, creaking audibly as she did so, clearing away the evidence of their having been there, her face ashen at the thought of that terrible threat.

Schulze hesitated no longer. 'See them cows out there,' he indicated the half-dozen skinny cattle grazing in front of the cottage. They nodded.

'Well, we're gonna belly-crawl to them. If we can use them as cover, we can move to that ditch beyond. It leads straight into the woods. With a bit o' luck we'll make it without being spotted. All right, Matz, off you go, and you, too, fly-boy.' Schulze shot the terrified old crone one last threatening look and cried, 'Remember, I'll ram it in till yer eyes pop!' and then he was off after the others, wriggling furiously towards the cows, while the partisan skirmish line came ever closer.

Surprisingly enough, the animals didn't panic as the three

humans appeared so unexpectedly at their feet, but continued chewing the cud placidly, looking at the men with their big brown stupid eyes as if they were of no significance. Indeed they were so tame that Matz narrowly escaped being urinated upon, as one of them lifted its tail and directed a jet of steaming yellow liquid at the spot where he had crouched only a moment before. *'Pissed on on active service!'* he complained later, 'by a frigging bovine cow. Ain't there no end to the horrors of this frigging war?' But at this moment he was too concerned with escaping from the French partisans to worry about the indignity of his narrow escape.

The three of them crawled slowly with the cows, trying to reach the ditch before the partisans spotted them. They were quite close. They could hear them calling to one another and later Schulze would swear that they were close enough for him to catch 'the stink of all that garlic they have to eat 'cos everybody knows the frogs only make love with their mouths.' Schulze, bringing up the rear, could hear the slurping noise cows make when they drink water and guessed that the first one must have reached the ditch. He raised his head and chanced a look. The partisans were only a hundred metres away. It was now or never.

'Into the water,' he hissed. 'Let's go. They'll be on to us in half a mo!'

Almost noiselessly they slipped into the muddy water while the cows drank and began to wriggle along the ditch. It was tough going and within seconds Schulze was sweating hard in spite of the cold water. Progress was made more difficult by the fact that the ditch ran uphill and they were constantly losing their grip and slipping downwards. Indeed, Schulze had just managed to prevent himself slithering back a second time when Matz in the lead hissed, *'Frog! Duck!'*

As one they submerged themselves in the murky water, as somewhere to their front there was the slapping sound of one of the partisans wading through the water. Schulze kept his head under water, his lungs threatening to burst but a moment later the Maquis had passed and Schulze thrust his head above the water, chest heaving as he sucked in air greedily.

'Hell's teeth!' Matz gasped. 'First a cow nearly pisses on me and now a frog puts his frigging foot right in the small o' me back!' He spluttered indignantly.

'Couldn't happen to a nicer bloke,' Schulze snapped, regaining his breath. 'Now move it agen before some frog puts his frigging frog foot right up yer skinny ass.'

Five minutes later they emerged from the ditch, stinking, sweating and covered in mud. Cautiously Schulze peered down into the valley. The Maquis were in the farmyard and even at that distance he could hear the old crone's yells as they beat her up.

'Come on,' he urged. 'Won't be long before the old bag'll be singing like a canary.' He thrust his way into the thick lines of firs, followed by the other two, knowing that they had to make the most of their advantage before the Maquis took up the chase.

Behind them the first excited shots rang out as some over-enthusiastic Maquis loosed off his rifle; the old woman had told her tale. Schulze frowned. Either they made it, he told himself grimly, or they stood and made a fight for it. Frau Schulze's handsome son was not going to betray what was left of SS Assault Regiment Wotan to those murderous bastards. 'Come on,' he urged, 'the cunts are on to us.'

CHAPTER 5

'Captain, let's get a few things straight from the start,' Colonel Petersen said as they faced each other across the office desk. 'You know the kind of treatment coloured soldiers receive in the US Army today and you know that High Command thinks that coloured soldiers are only fit to be cooks and drivers, that sort of thing – the camp's shit shovellers,' he added a little bitterly, his thin, highly strung face angry under the neat crew-cut.

Wolf nodded but said nothing. Colonel Petersen was obviously a typical, high-minded liberal of the East Coast variety. It must be tough for him in the US Army, Wolf told himself, where the black was little more than a third-class citizen.

'But Captain, remember this, all my men – note that I don't call them "boys" – are volunteers for the infantry. Yes, I said *volunteers*!' Petersen's grey eyes behind nickel-rimmed GI glasses were hard and challenging, almost as if he expected the man facing him to make some snide remark. But Wolf remained silent. He was beginning to like Colonel 'Black Jack' Petersen.

'All my noncoms and junior officers are black. Only myself and my company commanders are white. So when this battalion goes operational, it will be nearly ninety-nine per cent black.' Petersen leaned forward, his voice suddenly emotional. 'And by God they are going to prove to those damned bigots out there that the black soldier *will* and *can* fight!'

'They're naturally inexperienced in combat, sir?' Wolf ventured.

'Of course they are, Captain. As green as the growing corn. But they'll learn and they'll fight. Hell, blacks have fought in the ranks of the American Army ever since the revolutionary war. Do you know, Wolf, the first American serviceman to be killed in action in this war was a black man, though no one knew it at the time because he passed as a white. I'm talking of Robert Brooks who was killed by the Japs in the Philippines back in 'forty-two. Why our own commanding general, General Devers of Sixth US Army Group, named a parade ground at Fort Knox after him. Oh, I know they call me "Black Jack" Petersen behind my back. But I'm proud of the nickname. It was also given to General Pershing, Commander-in-Chief in France in the old war, because he once commanded the Tenth Cavalry, also black, just like my own 600th Infantry Battalion.' He stopped and forced a thin smile. When he spoke again, his voice was less passionate, more under control. 'So you see, Captain Wolf, I am something of a fanatic in matters concerning my soldiers.'

Wolf returned the smile. As a Jew and a homosexual, he knew what prejudice meant. Now he knew he *really* liked Colonel 'Black Jack' Petersen. The Colonel was obviously a man of high principle; but, a cynical little voice said at the back of his mind, 'principles don't shoot SS men!'

'Well, sir, if you'll allow me, I'd like to brief you on the mission. Higher Headquarters think it's vital that we set off as soon as possible. Top Brass is really worried about the purpose of these SS guys in the High Vosges.'

'Okay, Captain, shoot!' Petersen said, very business-like now.

Wolf walked across to the big map of Eastern France pinned on the wall of Petersen's office. 'Alsace, sir.' He swept his delicate little hand down the length of France's frontier with the Reich. 'Ninety per cent of the natives are German-speaking and I would guess that perhaps fifty per cent of those are German sympathisers. Here, around Colmar, there are some one hundred thousand German soldiers of the German 19th Army bottled up and besieged by the French Army, which is a strictly snafu outfit,' he added grimly.

'Situation normal, all fucked up!' Petersen spelled out the GI term.

'Exactly. The French can hold them at Colmar but they can't take them. So we have a theoretically dangerous situation, a kind of Trojan Horse right in our midst. What worried Higher Command at this moment is this. Are the Krauts going to take advantage of the 19th Army and a potential loyal civilian population? If they counter-attacked in Alsace, it would mean that our vital railroad communications with the ports would be cut so that our armies in France and Belgium would be dangerously undersupplied. The recapture of Alsace would be a tremendous propaganda boost for the German home population. And,' he hesitated a moment, as if even he, the trained Intelligence officer, hardly dared speak aloud what he was thinking, 'it might well mean de Gaulle's government in Paris would fall and the whole Allied coalition fall apart. Jesus Christ, sir,' he said desperately, 'A German attack into Alsace could well put back the end of the war another year.' He looked hard at a bewildered, worried Petersen and said emphatically, 'It's as bad as that, Colonel!'

For a moment Petersen was lost for words, but finally he broke the silence and asked, 'Okay, so what role do these missing SS men play?'

'That's what we're about to find out, sir. My informants tell me that they are in no great strength, perhaps some two hundred of them in all, and they have no heavy weapons nor vehicles, though, mind you, up there in the High Vosges vehicles might well be a hindrance.'

'We would outnumber them four to one then, Wolf?'

'Yes sir. But don't kid yourself. These SS jerks are tough hombres. They know their way around; they're combat-wise veterans, and you're facing them with completely green soldiers, however brave and determined they might be.'

Petersen nodded and said, 'Now where exactly are they located, these SS?'

Wolf touched the map with his forefinger. 'They were last spotted in the mountains here, north of Gerardmer, heading in a north-easterly direction. Ste Marie-aux-Mines, here, is the nearest town on the approximate line of march, though undoubtedly they will swing round it, bearing generally eastwards into the really rugged terrain up there.'

'Is this Ste Marie-aux-Mines held by Allied forces?'

'No sir. Just a handful of overage French gendarmes, and,' he hesitated momentarily, 'a laundry unit responsible for washing for the men in the line down on the plain below. Perhaps twenty or so soldiers supervising the local French labour they employ.'

'Black?'

'Yes, black sir.'

'Another bunch of black shit-shovellers,' Petersen said without rancour, his brow creased in thought.

'Yes sir. But I doubt if they're beefing up there, with the whole town to themselves and no Jin Crows or rednecks around, if you follow my meaning, sir.'

'Dames, French dames?'

Wolf nodded.

Petersen dismissed the problem of black soldiers making love to white women with an airy wave of his hand and Wolf grinned to himself. One could tell he was a northern liberal. If he had been a southerner, he would be reaching for the lynching rope at the very thought of a 'nigger' bedding a white woman. 'Listen, if you were the German commander up there on the run, or so it seems, perhaps short of food and water etc, what might you do at Ste Marie-aux-Mines?' His eyes behind the nickel-rimmed glasses stared into Wolf's face. 'Well come on, Captain, try to put yourself into the boots of that SS commander.'

Wolf tugged the end of his nose thoughtfully. 'I see what you're getting at. If the SS commander is desperate enough and has recced the situation at Ste Marie-aux-Mines through spies, he might well attempt to take what he needed from the town.'

'That's my thinking too, Wolf. So if we could get there *before* them,' he said, 'the Krauts would be walking straight into a nice little trap and my men would be able to prove just what they were worth – *from a fortified defensive position*! What do you think of that?'

Wolf considered for a moment. Outnumbered as they were, the SS troopers were more than a match for Petersen's unblooded battalion. But if his blacks were fighting from prepared positions and took the SS by surprise, then things might well be very different. They would stand a good chance of beating the Germans.

'I agree with your thinking, sir,' Wolf said after a moment, 'but what happens if the Krauts *don't* attempt to take Ste Marie-aux-Mines? What then?'

Petersen grinned but there was no warmth in his grey eyes behind the GI glasses. 'Then, my friend, Higher Headquarters will be able to do what they have been wanting to do for a long time. I'm told I'm something of a thorn in their flesh. They'll have "Black Jack" Petersen's arse in a sling and his "coons" can go back to shit-shovelling where the Top Brass thinks they belong. If we fail to outguess the Krauts on this one . . .' he hesitated for a moment, 'it will be the end of the Sixth's short, and so far not very glorious, career. They'll can us just like that!' He clicked his fingers.

The strength of Petersen's feeling animated Wolf as if someone had just given him a shot of dope. The old cynicism and general war-weariness vanished and he felt as he had done back in '41 when he enlisted just after Pearl Harbor. Then he had experienced a sense of purpose, a feeling that he, and many other Americans, were setting out on some sort of crusade against the evil of fascism; that there was a job to be done to eradicate an evil from the world which would be a better place thereafter.

'Colonel,' he said, carried away by his new-found enthusiasm, 'you can count on me! You and your Battalion will have my fullest support.'

Petersen grinned and stretched out his hand. Wolf took it and was surprised by just how hard it was. 'Welcome aboard, Wolf,' he rasped. 'Welcome to Black Jack Petersen's coons.'

In the outer office Top Sergeant Washington Lee the Third frowned and leaned back in his chair. He knew and trusted the Colonel, although he was a white man and the handsome top kick had a profound distrust of white men in general. Of course, he looked forward to going into action with the battalion. Hell, that was why he had given up a nice easy number with the Service of Supply in 'Gay Paree'. But he hadn't bargained with having to fight the SS in his first combat mission. Lazily he raised his black bulk from his chair and, walking across the room, stared at his image in the fly-blown mirror. The face – bright, sharp eyes, clean profile, tough aggressive chin – could have come straight from a recruiting poster for the US Army, save for one thing – the features were coal black and the US Army did not feature black recruiting posters in 1944.

His frown deepened as he considered what lay before them now. He was confident he wouldn't turn yellow in combat. He grinned at the thought of a negro turning yellow. Nor would most of the senior noncoms. But he wasn't so sure of the rank-and-file. Most of them were young bucks from the South, with little education and little self-confidence in themselves in spite of their physique and training. All their lives they had been taught by those rednecks south of the Mason-Dixon Line that black self-confidence could lead only to trouble – a kick in the ass, or, even worse, the mob and the lynching rope! How would young men like that, who were considered as third-class citizens to be hustled off the sidewalk even by their own people, stand up to the pressure of combat? How would they be able to fight against white men, especially when those white men were from the SS?

'Brother,' Sergeant Washington Lee whistled softly at his own image in the mirror, 'this one is gonna be a beaut, a real beaut!'

He let his big hand fall to the forty-five pistol strapped to his hip, the thongs from the holster tied to his thigh in the fashion of an old-time western gun-slinger. The feel of the cold metal butt gave him a sense of reassurance. Lead talked more powerfully than words, he told himself. As long as he was still on his feet and could hold the pistol, there'd be none of that black trash running away from the enemy and letting the C.O. down. 'No sir,' he said to himself in the manner of lonely men, 'so long as First Sergeant Washington Lee can fire a forty-five, ole Black Jack Petersen's coons is gonna stand and fight.'

CHAPTER 6

'Machine-gunner,' von Dodenburg hissed, 'stand by to fire.'

'Sir,' the tense, white-faced youngster crouched behind the MG 42, snapped back, cocking the action automatically. Next to him in the bushes his number two prepared to feed the long belt of ammunition into the breech.

Von Dodenburg flashed a look to left and right. The prospect of a battle had pumped new energy into his half-starved, weary men. They crouched in their positions, all fear vanished from their thin unshaven faces, eyes flashing keenly. He nodded his approval. They were behaving in the best tradition of the SS; they wouldn't let him down. But after this, he told himself, if they got through safely, he would see they were fed and rested before they continued their long trek back to the Reich.

'Hold your fire till I give the command,' he hissed, as the sound of many feet thrashing through the undergrowth towards their hiding place came ever closer.

'*Hold your fire till the C.O. orders . . . hold your fire . . .*' the command went down the line to left and right.

Von Dodenburg raised himself on one knee, his trigger finger cocked, feeling the comforting hardness of the Schmeisser tucked against his right hip. It wouldn't be long now and he could guess who was coming – those damned Maquis who had been pursuing them for nearly a week now! Somehow he had to teach them such a sharp lesson this time that they would stop for good. His exhausted young troopers, living off a couple of slices of bread and a pinch or two of *Traubenzucker**, washed down with a swig of water from their canteens, couldn't stand the pace much longer. Sooner or later they'd crack.

---

* A dextrose product, used to produce instant energy

The noise was getting ever closer. Von Dodenburg swallowed. A thin sweat was trickling slowly and unpleasantly down the small of his back. His breath was coming in short, sharp gasps as if he were running a race. Angrily, he told himself to stop it, but a moment later he was panting again.

There was the sound of breaking branches to his right. He jerked up his head, eyes narrowed to slits, face set and determined. 'Attention three o'clock,' he ordered.

'*Attention three o'clock . . . attention . . .*' Again the order was whispered down the line of tense expectant young men. He could hear the soft click of metal on stone as the riflemen altered their sightings. It wouldn't be long now, he told himself, before the crazy cruel game with its lethal outcome commenced.

A sudden flurry of green branches. Someone cursed angrily. Less than a hundred metres away a big burly figure blundered into the open, trailing broken twigs behind him. Von Dodenburg raised his Schmeisser automatically, then let it drop the very next instant. 'Schulze, you horned ox,' he cried, 'where in three devils' name have you been?'

'They're after us, sir,' Schulze cried back, his chest heaving, as Matz burst into the open, dragging with him a third man, clutching a case.

'Over here, *quick*!' von Dodenburg yelled. 'We're waiting for them!'

Schulze shook his head, gasping violently for breath. 'No sir. We'll keep running . . . lead them across your front . . . You can pop 'em as they come by.'

'But Schulze, you horned ox, that might be suicide' – the words died on von Dodenburg's lips.

Schulze was already running, followed by the other two, staggering as if they were drunk. Von Dodenburg cursed and then told himself the big insubordinate bastard was risking his life to save the rest of Wotan. He dared not throw that last chance away. 'Prepare to fire!' he commanded as the noise of the pursuers came ever closer.

All along the waiting line men were slipping off their

safety-catches, closing one eye and peering through their sights as they prepared to fire. The suspense was almost unbearable.

Von Dodenburg raised his Schmeisser. He prayed that the whole bunch would come blundering into the opening like the untrained rabble they were; then they could finish them off in one tremendous volley. Now they were almost there. He could hear their excited calls to one another and the noise their feet made as they stumbled and crashed through the undergrowth.

'*Ils sont la – les sales cons*!' someone cried as the first Maquis burst into the open and spotted the three running figures only a hundred metres or so away.

'Hold your fire!' von Dodenburg hissed as more and more of the black-bereted little men came running out of the trees, most of them walking arsenals, weapons of all kinds hanging from virtually every part of their body. He began to count. He got to a hundred, all clustered together, perhaps waiting for an order to continue the chase, and knew he could wait no longer. Already the leaders were bending on one knee and snapping off aimed shots at the three figures, clearly visible in the open. Any second now they would get lucky and that would be the end of Schulze and his running-mate, Matz.

'*FEUER*!' he yelled and at the same instant pressed the trigger of his automatic, feeling the Schmeisser beginning to pump lead at his hip.

What happened next was not war. It was murder. As the three running men dropped to the ground, knowing they would be hunted no more, the hidden Wotan troopers blasted into the Maquis. They hadn't a chance. At that short range even the poorest shot couldn't miss.

Suddenly the surprised Fenchmen were galvanized into violent action as that first volley slammed into them. They went down by the score, arms flailing the air as if they were scaling the rungs of an invisible ladder, shrieking in sheer agony, dead before they hit the ground. Some tried to break out of the trap, but the Wotan troopers, carried away by that

savage animal blood-lust of battle, didn't give them a chance.
They were mown down before they had gone a few metres.
Now there was a living carpet of shattered human beings,
writhing and twisting in their final agonies.

But still the SS men continued to fire, knowing that this
time they were going to wipe out the men who had hunted
them so doggedly this last week, and that on the slaughter of
the Maquis depended their own safety. Von Dodenburg, his
face contorted, eyes glittering with almost sexual excitement,
continued firing with the rest, swinging from the hips like a
western gunfighter, mowing them down without any mercy;
giving rein at last to that burning anger that had been his
sole motivating force during the long chase in the mountains.

There was a dry click. At his hip the Schmeisser ceased its
cruel song of death. For a moment he stared vacantly down at
it, as if he could not understand why it had stopped firing.
Abruptly it dawned on him. He had emptied his magazine;
he had run out of ammunition and his men would also if they
didn't stop wasting their bullets so purposelessly. The Maquis
were finished. They had been so effectively trapped that there
were only a handful left crawling away to the cover of the
trees, dragging their bloodied broken limbs behind them.
'Cease firing!' he called hoarsely above the angry crackle of
the small arms fire. *'CEASE FIRING!'*

For what seemed an age nothing happened. The troopers
were still carried away by the blood-lust of battle, working
their bolts automatically, firing into the writhing mass of
dead and dying Frenchmen piled up in front of them in the
forest glade. Then, slowly, their senses began to return. The
firing petered away and finally ceased altogether. That
awesome place of slaughter was silent, save for a long
lingering echo which seemed to go on for ever.

Von Dodenburg looked at the mound of dead Frenchmen,
slaughtered so cruelly, and the few wounded survivors trying
to crawl for safety. He knew what he had to do, but still he
hated it. He still hesitated. Inside him a little voice said,

'Kuno, don't be a bloody fool. It's either them or you, and never fear they would have done much worse to you if you'd have fallen into their hands. *Now move!*'

He cleared his throat. 'Out you men over there; search the bodies for food and ammo. I'll see to the wounded myself.' Slowly and deliberately he fixed a new magazine into his machine pistol. He tapped it to check that it was firmly in place, then snapped the catch from automatic to single shot. Equally slowly he walked towards the first of the French wounded, hating what he was going to have to do.

Schulze, sitting slumped on the littered ground, exhausted from the long chase, watched him go. Next to him the little *Luftwaffe* pilot watched too, his face puzzled. 'What's your C.O. going to do, sarge?' Schulze didn't answer, but Matz did.

'Well, he ain't gonna serve a cup o' china tea on a silver platter, flyboy,' he growled, as if he were angry that the pilot had even raised the question.

Von Dodenburg paused in front of the first of the French wounded: a flaxen-haired kid, whose left leg was a shattered crimson stump through which the bone glistened like polished ivory. Slowly, awfully slowly, he raised his Schmeisser and pressed the muzzle against the boy's temple. The kid looked up at him without fear, as if he were resigned to his fate; as if he had always expected that this was the way he would end. No sound escaped his lips.

Squatting there, the three of them could see how von Dodenburg's trigger finger whitened as he began to take first pressure.

Next to Schulze the pilot gasped, 'Oh my God, he's going to shoot the frog kid!'

'What did you frigging well think?' Schulze sneered, his face bitter. 'Give him a frigging pat on the frigging back for a frigging good . . .'

Schulze's outburst was drowned by the crack of a single shot. The boy's skull seemed to burst apart like a soft-boiled egg tapped too heavily. Blood spurted out from a dozen cracks. Slowly the boy's face began to drip down to his skinny chest like molten wax.

'Why?' the pilot moaned, close to tears as von Dodenburg, face resolute but absolute, strode over to the next wounded Frenchman. 'Why?'

'I'll tell yer fucking *why*!' Matz snorted. 'Because out here it's dog eat dog. We don't want any of them friggers shopping us later. So we waste them. Oh, fuck it!' He picked up a stone and then threw it aimlessly away again like a man whose exasperation was too much to bear. The pilot watched in horrified fascination as von Dodenburg finished off the Frenchmen one by one until they were all dead; while his young troopers looted the bodies, whooping and crying like excited school children when they found a packet of cigarettes, a slice of bread or a sausage. Finally he turned and began to wade through the dead, his face stern and unrevealing heading for the three men still squatting on the grass. Hastily Schulze and Matz rose to their feet, followed a little more slowly by the pilot, his mind in a whirl, heart thumping crazily, as he realized in what a brutal world he now found himself.

The tall, hard-faced SS Colonel must have realized what he was thinking, for as the three of them clicked to attention and saluted, he rasped, 'Welcome to Wotan, Sergeant. This,' he extended a hand to indicate the dead Frenchmen lying everywhere in the grotesque extravagant poses of those done to death violently, 'is the way we do it in the SS.' He smiled.

'Yes sir. Of course, sir!' the pilot stuttered and wished fervently he had never become involved in this crazy mission.

Von Dodenburg dismissed him and turned to Schulze and Matz, 'All right, you two rogues; don't try to blind me with bullshit pretending you are soldiers. Stand at ease.'

The two relaxed, while the still horrified pilot tried to keep his gaze off the scene of the massacre.

'Now then, what's been going off since the two of you did your disappearing act? Without my orders, I must point out.'

'Well, sir, we were just doing a bit of a private reconnaissance . . .' 'Cut out the lies, you horned ox!' von Dodenburg interrupted him sharply. 'I know your *bits of private reconnaissance*! Out looking for as much sauce as you could loot and hopefully a willing wench to cock your leg over. Now get on with it. How did you find our friend from the *Luftwaffe* here?'

Swiftly Schulze told the big Colonel what had happened and then indicated the now battered briefcase which the little pilot was still carrying. 'There's some kind of orders for us in there, sir,' he concluded.

Von Dodenburg looked at him in mock incredulity. 'And you mean to say that all this time you haven't tried to get your greedy paws on what's inside it, Schulze?' He shook his head, as if in disbelief.

'It's locked, sir, and the flyboy here ain't got the key. Besides the frogs was after us all the time.'

'I'll accept your apology, Schulze.' For the first time that day von Dodenburg grinned. 'All right then, shall we have a look-see at what our dearly beloved Reichsheini* has sent us?' He turned and called to the nearest trooper, happily munching a bar of chocolate he had taken from the dead, the paper cover stained with its former owner's blood. 'Hey, you, stop feeding your guts. Unsheath your nail-file and get over here at the double!'

A moment later, an impatient Schulze had inserted the trooper's bayonet inside the briefcase's flap and begun to force it open.

* Nickname for Himmler

CHAPTER 7

'It doesn't look as if the natives are friendly, Wolf,' Colonel Petersen commented wrily as the leading half-track started to clatter down the steep, cobbled road that led into the mountain-top mining village of Ste Marie-aux-Mines. Captain Wolf took his eyes off the sombre-faced civilians lining the pavement on both sides of the main road and nodded. 'Most of them over the age of twenty-five will have been German-born, Colonel,' he explained. 'And all of them will have menfolk in the *Wehrmacht*. After all, until we came a month ago, this was regarded as part of Germany.'

Petersen nodded and said, 'We'll have to ensure our security is one hundred per cent then.'

'Yes,' Wolf agreed, as the driver swung the half-track round a corner, following the sign which read '*Eighth Base Laundry Section, US Army*'. 'No doubt the krauts will have agents here.'

'Willya get a load of that bull, Colonel,' Sergeant Washington Lee cried in disgust, as he spotted the sign planted below the main one. '*We aim to please*! What crap. Typical rear echelon feather merchants. One man in the line and five to bring up the coca-cola. *We aim to please*!' He spat contemptuously over the side of the vehicle.

Wolf grinned. In the US Army you were always being 'allowed' to cross bridges, have your teeth fixed, your shoes fixed, etc etc, by courtesy of some goddam outfit or other. Every jerk-off wanted his bit of personal publicity, it seemed.

Petersen's face remained serious, however, as the US post came into view, guarded by a sloppy black sentry, his helmet liner tilted to one side, leaning on his rifle as if it were a crutch.

'Well, somebody's got to do the laundry, Sergeant. Everybody has his part to play, however humble, in this war, you know.' The NCO was not impressed.

The sentry spotted the silver eagle on Colonel Petersen's helmet and came to attention. As an afterthought he raised his rifle as if he might salute and then thought better of it. Instead he said brightly, all yellow eyes and brilliant white teeth, 'Morning you all, colonel suh!'

Sergeant Washington Lee groaned and slapped his forehead as if he couldn't believe the evidence of his own eyes. For his part Colonel Petersen said, 'Better shape up, soldier. You might be a laundryman, but remember you're a soldier too.'

But the sentry wasn't listening. His eyes were growing larger and larger as more and more vehicles appeared, all filled with black soldiers. 'Holy cow, Colonel suh!' he exclaimed, 'you got the whole goddam black army with you, suh!' At that even Petersen allowed himself a wintry grin.

Five minutes later the companies, bayonets fixed and weighed down with equipment, started to move out to the outskirts of the mountain village to occupy the heights to the north and the two steep passes which led in and out of the place, watched by those sombre-faced villagers who were keeping their thoughts about so many black soldiers appearing in their midst to themselves. Even the kids, unusually for France, refrained from pestering the soldiers with their usual cries for 'chocolate, cigarettes for papa . . . and candy.'

Colonel Petersen and Wolf got down to preparing the place for a German attack, aided by the commander of the laundry, an extremely fat second-lieutenant who perspired a great deal and smiled nervously to reveal a mouthful of gold teeth.

'If they come,' Petersen reasoned, 'my guess is that they'll do so over the ground to the south of Ste Marie. It's not so rugged. They won't take the roads, being experienced troops, and they won't swing in from the high ground to the north. Hence my dispositions – here, here and here,' he stabbed the map with a bony forefinger, 'are based on denying them the heights and observation posts. I figure they'll assume the town is only lightly held and will risk the gamble, not knowing that three-quarters of my battalion will be located outside the place.'

The laundry commander mopped his black brow nervously with a khaki handkerchief and asked hesitantly, 'And what role do my boys play, sir?'

Colonel Petersen smiled at him. 'Your guys are going to be the bait, Lieutenant.'

'The bait, sir?' The man's jowls wobbled with fear.

Wolf grinned. The laundry commander was obviously not one of 'Petersen's Fighting Coons', as the men of the 600th were already beginning to call themselves, now that they were virtually in combat. He smelled of fear.

'Yes, your fellers will go about their business down here as if everything was completely normal. To any Kraut observer or patrol you'll seem to be a rear-line outfit, who have no idea that the war is going to catch up with them.'

The laundry commander swallowed hard, his moonlike face glistening with fear. 'Is it . . . is it gonna catch up with us?' he stuttered.

'It's just a manner of speaking,' Petersen soothed him, as Sergeant Washington Lee at the back of the room said to himself contemptuously, 'That nigger's gonna cream his goddam skivvies any moment now.'

'Fat Anna' frowned as she watched Louis, the laundry officer, engaged in conversation with these strange warlike black soldiers who had appeared so surprisingly in this sleepy little backwater. Anna was an Alsatian woman in her late thirties, blonde and plump with a permanently vague look, though she was not altogether so. Ever since the *Amis* had arrived she had been Louis's 'personal' laundry woman, which entailed her picking up his washing once a week; a very noisy business with lots of creaking springs, giggles and some strange stifled sheeplike braying from the fat black officer in moments of ecstasy.

Later Anna would emerge, his washing in a bundle over her shoulder, her apron pockets bulging with Hershey bars, packs of Chesterfields and cans of C rations, promising that she would return the following week to help the Lieutenant 'pack up his washing'.

But the fat Alsatian woman's heart really wasn't in it. As she would often complain to her aged mother, 'He's a great burden to bear for me, Mama.' Something about which her mother could only agree when she had seen Louis's great black bulk. But with three small children to feed and a husband somewhere on the Russian front in the *Wehrmacht*, Fat Anna had no other choice than to 'collect Louis's laundry' every week.

Yet she resented the snide remarks of the other women, the barely concealed scornful looks and malicious whispers of 'fancy letting a black negro stick his thing into her'; and the like. Lately she had become a little alarmed, too, as the persistent rumours began to mount in the little town that the Germans were coming back. Soon a great new counter-attack would begin which would throw the Amis out of Alsace again. What would happen to her when the gentlemen of the Gestapo, in their leather coats and green felt hats, returned? She doubted that they would be content with just shearing off her blonde locks as a 'collaborator'. With a husband serving on the Russian front, they might well regard her as a traitor for having associated with an *Ami*, and a black one to boot.

'Fat Anna's' frown deepened as she watched Louis, sweating even more than normal, his fat face revealing his fear only too clearly. There was something going on, she told herself, something to do with the returning Germans, and that something could cause trouble for herself and her brood if she didn't take care. But what could she do?

She tucked her empty laundry bag under her arm once more, guessing that on this particular September day Louis wouldn't want her to help him 'pack up his washing'. Thoughtfully she wandered out of the gate a few moments later, oblivious to the wolf whistles of the black soldiers in the waiting trucks. What was she going to do?

*

The question of what to do next troubled von Dodenburg at precisely that same moment as he crouched with his men in the woods to the south of Ste Marie-aux-Mines. His orders, which had been contained in the dead officer's briefcase, had been signed by Himmler himself. He was to avoid all centres of population, however pro-German, and head straight for the 'Crest Route'.

'That's what the French call it,' he had explained to his men, once he had digested Himmler's orders. 'During World War One when our *Gebirgsjager** and the French Alpine troops fought it out in the High Vosges, French engineers built a secret road along the peak line following a route which had been worked out by the Roman legions when they marched that way northwards. Their aim had been to surprise our people – and they succeeded. After 1918 the Route became something of a tourist attraction for French motorists who owned cars capable of making the steep gradients, almost one in three in some places. Now, however, with all civilian travel by car banned due to the rationing of petrol, the *Reichsführer*'s advisers think the Crest Route will not be in use. They feel, too, that there should not be any enemy military traffic up there, and, besides, once the first snow begins to fall the Route is generally regarded as impassable for vehicular traffic.'

'But what are we going to do when we get up there, sir?' Schulze had objected, airing the views of the others.

Von Dodenburg dodged the question, knowing that his men had been placed under enough strain, since they had escaped from Montélimar. Besides, he wasn't too sure himself what the second part of Himmler's orders implied. So he had lied to them, answering, '*Reichsführer SS* thinks that the Crest Route is the best and safest way for us to pass through Alsace and reach our own lines in the Saar.'

That had satisfied them and thereafter he had noted that the men's spirits had picked up considerably at the thought

* German alpine troops

that they were going to escape from American-held territory without any further combat.

But as they crouched there, von Dodenburg eyed the white peaks which were the Crest Route in the far distance and he knew that his men wouldn't last without some good food inside them. The only place to find it before they entered the High Vosges was Ste Marie-aux-Mines.

Schulze, squatting next to him, read his thoughts, and said, 'Sir, do you want me and Matz to have a look-see?' He rubbed his unshaven jaw with a hand like a small steam shovel. 'If anyone can find a bit o' grub for those greenbeaks it's us.'

'Yes, and fill your guts with sauce and suds at the same time as well, I shouldn't wonder.'

'A soldier's life is awful hard, sir,' Schulze said with a mock whine. 'There ain't many pleasures left for a poor stubble-hopper, 'cept a modest half-litre o' beer or perhaps a teeny drop o' schnapps.'

'My heart bleeds for you, Schulze,' von Dodenburg said unfeelingly. 'What a delicate, suffering little soul you must be. Now listen.' Suddenly his voice had iron in it. 'I want us to go in fast and leave the same way. It doesn't look as if the place is occupied by the *Amis*. But there will be French police and I don't want them to have time to alert the nearest enemy army post. So quick's the word and sharp's the action. Got it?

'Got it, sir!'

'You see that steeple?' Von Dodenburg pointed to the church just visible on the horizon. 'I want you and Matz to take a small patrol and head for it. If everything goes all right, you fire a green flare – here, take my Very pistol.' He pulled the ugly-looking flare pistol from his belt and handed it to Schulze. 'We'll be waiting on the outskirts. As soon as we see your signal, we're in, loot as much food as we can find and then we swing out into that high ground to north. See it?'

Schulze nodded dutifully. 'See it, sir,' he growled and then asked hesitantly, 'But what if we run into trouble, sir, what then?'

'*Then*, you big-horned ox, you pick up your hind legs, tuck them under your arms and run like hell!' von Dodenburg replied.

Schulze was not impressed by the C.O.'s answer. He looked around at the weary emaciated young men sitting slumped on the ground and frowned, 'Well, sir, I don't think this lot of Christmas tree soldiers will be doing much more running. They're buggered!'

Now it was von Dodenburg's turn to frown. He realized just how right the big noncom was. The 'Christmas tree soldiers', as he called them, couldn't – wouldn't – run much more. If they didn't get food soon, and plenty of it, he would never be able to lead them to *Schloss* Falkenstein and whatever mysterious mission that awaited them there. It was almost the end of the line for SS Assault Regiment Wotan.

Over Ste Marie-aux-Mines the sun slowly began to set, colouring the mountains a sinister blood-red hue. Suddenly Colonel Kuno von Dodenburg shivered, as if overcome by an abrupt feeling of foreboding.

BOOK TWO

The Fighting Coons

'The Negro soldier's first taste of warfare in World War II was on army posts right here in his own country. This caused considerable confusion in the minds of the draftees as to who the enemy really was.'

Black Colonel Howard Donovan Queen, US Army.

CHAPTER 1

The Führer farted once again. Marshal Keitel looked embarrassed, or as embarrassed as that wooden-faced soldier ever could look. Next to him, Colonel-General Jodl went even paler than normal, fighting to prevent himself from gagging at the nauseating stench. Adolf Hitler, the man who commanded the destiny of the Third Reich, appeared not to notice. But then he broke wind constantly, due to the sixty pills, many of them laxatives, which he swallowed daily. Instead he stared once more at the huge map of the Western Front which covered one wall of the room. Next to him his Alsatian bitch, Blondi, growled softly, as if impatient to be taken on her daily walk. But this morning Hitler was not going to be hurried. He had been mulling the great idea over in his head for days now. This morning he was going to spring it on his closest military advisers and test their reactions. Outside there was no sound save for the steady tramp of jackboots on the gravelled paths. Since the attempt on his life the previous July, Hitler made sure that he was constantly protected by guards.

Jodl cleared his throat. The work was piling up in his office. With Germany's defences collapsing on all sides and her armies in retreat on both the western and eastern fronts, there were a hundred and one orders to be issued. He hadn't the time to waste while the Führer waited for inspiration.

Slowly Hitler turned round and once more Jodl was shocked by his appearance – the stooped shoulders, the shaky hands, the slack mouth, the blue eyes watery and distant. Nevertheless the depression of the summer had vanished. In spite of his physical infirmity, the Führer remained confident.

'Jodl,' he said slowly, 'once more please. The situation on the Western Front, *Herr Generaloberst*.'

Inwardly Jodl groaned. Outwardly he gave Hitler a cold

smile and rasped, '*Jawohl, mein Führer!*' Swiftly, in that highly complicated manner of his, Jodl began to describe the impossible situation on the Western Front, with British, Canadian, American and French armies all poised to attack over the German border, once their supplies caught up with them:

'Emphasis seems to be on the Allied left wing . . . secondary concentrations on both sides of Aachen . . . lesser emphasis on the battle area of Nancy and the southern Vosges front.' On and on the litany of doom continued.

Surprisingly, Hitler did not seem to mind. He simply listened, hands shaking, as if he were afflicted with the palsy, nodding his head from time to time, as if in agreement.

'From this situation,' Jodl continued, listening to himself talk and wondering why the Führer wanted to inflict this recital of gloom upon himself once more, 'we can assume that the Anglo-Canadians will attack from Holland into the Reich, while the Americans will assault the Siegfried line in the Aachen area. Patton's Third Army will also probably attack into the Saar, once it has dealt with the siege of Metz.' Jodl's voice petered away. There was no more to say.

Hitler farted.

A heavy silence descended upon the room, broken only by the steady tread of the sentry outside. Keitel tugged at his collar. Jodl examined his nails. Even Blondi growled no more, ears pricked up, as if she half-expected the Führer to make a personal appeal to her for. . . . For what? Jodl couldn't help thinking. Germany's position was hopeless. Any sane German knew that the only hope for the Reich now was to surrender on the best possible terms. But Adolf Hitler, he realized, was not a sane man. They continued to wait.

'*The Ardennes!*' Hitler announced, so abruptly that Jodl jumped, and Blondi jerked up her head.

'*Was haben Sie gesagt, mein Führer?*' Keitel barked.

'The Ardennes.' He raised one finger dramatically. 'I have made a momentous decision. I am taking the offensive. Here – out of the Ardennes!' He smashed his fist against the map, eyes blazing once more with the old fury, 'Across the Meuse and on to Antwerp!'

Jodl stared at him incredulously. His shoulders were squared, his eyes luminous and hypnotic, all signs of sickness and age vanished. Once again he was the old dynamic Hitler, the Führer of the great years of victory.

'*Grosser Gott!*' he rasped in his thick Austrian accent. 'If all goes well it could well be another Dunkirk. Twenty or thirty Anglo-American divisions annihilated, wiped off the map, the rest running for the Channel.'

Jodl listened open-mouthed as Hitler detailed his plan. A great wedge would be cut between the Allied armies as his own tanks raced for Antwerp to capture the enemy's major supply port on the continent. The panzer drive would cut off the armies at the front from their headquarters at the rear. He had done it before in Poland in 'thirty-nine and in France in 'forty. He would do it once again.

'*Meine Herren*,' he gasped, short of breath from so much excited talking, 'with luck – and luck is on the side of the bold – we could put Britain out of the war for a year. Then we could deal with Russia. Thereafter a negotiated peace, with favourable terms for our bloody but unbowed land.'

Keitel, lackey that he was, clapped his hands together like an excited schoolboy and cried with delight, 'Excellent, *mein Führer*. How typical of your genius that, at this eleventh hour, you should come up with such a brilliant scheme, which will undoubtedly turn the war in Germany's favour! *Grossartig!*' He beamed at a flushed Hitler, all fawning respect.

With difficulty Jodl concealed his disgust at his fellow officer's toadying. '*Mein Führer*,' he said quietly.

'Yes, Jodl?'

'With all due respect, may I point out that the concept is indeed brilliant and will undoubtedly catch the Americans by surprise in the Ardennes. After all, they are guarding a ninety-kilometre front with a single corps. Our troops would find it easy to break through a line held so thinly.'

Hitler's hectic enthusiasm increased. It seemed as if he had

THE HITLER PLAN

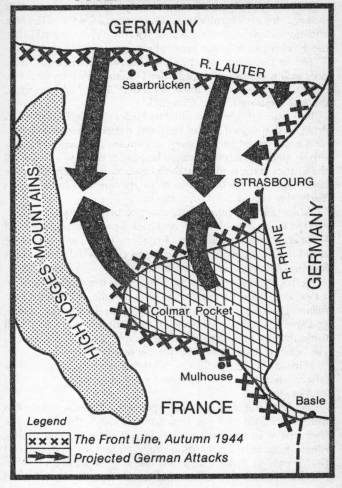

GERMANY

R. LAUTER

Saarbrücken

STRASBOURG

HIGH VOSGES MOUNTAINS

R. RHINE

GERMANY

Colmar Pocket

Mulhouse

Basle

FRANCE

Legend

× × × × The Front Line, Autumn 1944

→ Projected German Attacks

carried even the ever-sceptical Jodl with him. The pale-faced staff officer paused momentarily. Blondi looked up at him and growled. Jodl ignored both the dog and her master. He felt it was his sacred duty to Germany to prevent Hitler from going off the rails. He must not be allowed to throw away the Reich's last reserves in wild gambles.

'Have you considered Patton's Third Army, sir, down there in the Saar? What do you think Patton would do if we broke through in the Ardennes?' Jodl answered his own question before Hitler could object. 'Why, sir, he would swing his army around in the Saar and simply counter-attack on our southern flank. It would be typical of that cowboy general. We would be offering him the kind of opportunity that his flamboyant nature craves.' He stopped and waited for the expected outburst, but none came. Instead Hitler smiled softly at him and said, 'Why, of course, my dear Jodl, that is exactly what I would expect Patton to do and it is exactly what I would *want* him to do.'

'*Want him to do*, sir?' Jodl echoed stupidly.

'Yes.' Hitler turned to the map once more. 'Patton, here in the Saar, moves north to attack our flank. What follows? Do the Americans leave a great gap in their lines where his Third Army has been? Of course not; they fill the positions vacated by the Third with the troops of their Seventh Army, here in Alsace. The American Seventh Army will then be holding a line of the front once held by *two* American armies. They will be stretched to the limit.'

'Yes, *mein Führer*, but . . .' Jodl broke off. He could see that Hitler wasn't listening. His gaze was turned inwards, as if he were seeing some inner vision. Jodl realized that the Führer was thinking on his feet, improvising as he went along. 'Damn it!' he cursed to himself, Hitler was listening to his voices again.

'So,' Hitler continued, 'blow one is levelled against the enemy's thinly held positions in the Belgian Ardennes. His reaction is to thin out his line in French Alsace. What do we do?' He grinned at them, his face cunning and confident.

'Why, we launch blow two – *against their positions in Alsace*! Can't you see it, gentlemen? A pro-German Alsace actively helping our brave soldiers, a communist insurrection inland, the fall of the De Gaulle government, the collapse of the enemy's supply lines through France. Why, it could take France out of the war, too!' He took out his handkerchief with a hand that trembled violently and mopped his brow.

Jodl felt that the time had come for him to protest. 'But even if the Allied line in Alsace were to be thinned out, my Führer,' he objected, while Keitel stared at his highly polished boots, as if he were embarrassed by so much nonsense, 'the enemy will still be dug in behind the Rhine, and I don't need to tell you, sir, that the Rhine will be a major barrier for our troops.'

'*Aber, mein lieber Jodl*,' Hitler said in high good humour, as if he were not in the least offended by the staff officer's objection, 'initially there would be no need for our men to cross the Rhine.'

Jodl looked puzzled. Hitler beamed at him benevolently. 'You are forgetting the Colmar Pocket. General Weise has one hundred thousand men bottled up there. How easy would it be for him to break out of it and drive north for the glittering prize of Strasbourg, while, in the meantime, our little Trojan Horse trick rattles the Americans to the north. By the time they have woken up to the fact that it is only a feint, our troops will be crossing the Rhine north of Strasbourg in force.'

Jodl was too flabbergasted to speak. But Keitel, judging the time opportune, said, 'What, if I may ask, sir, is the Trojan Horse?' His face was flushed, as if he were embarrassed at his own temerity. Hastily, he added, 'What brilliant new scheme have you thought up, *mein Führer*? Please divulge it to us, sir.'

'As we have said, Keitel, there are thousands of honest citizens in Alsace now living under French tyranny who would gladly die for Germany, given the chance. What they lack is arms and organization. Given those two things, how effective they would be if,' he raised one finger dramatically, 'at the same time that Wiese breaks out of the Colmar Pocket, there were a popular uprising in Northern Alsace, with the civilians sabotaging American installations, barracks, signals systems, petrol dumps and so on. Why, in a flash the Americans would be fighting a two-front war. It would throw them into utter confusion.'

'But, sir, sir!' Jodl objected, trying to keep this absurd situation from getting even more out of hand, 'arms we could find for a popular uprising there, but where would we find the organization, the men to lead these untrained civilians? Most of their able-bodied men are in our *Wehrmacht* as it is. What is left *must* be boys or old men.'

'You are forgetting one thing, Jodl,' Hitler replied, again in no way offended by Jodl's objection.

'What is that, sir?' the other man asked somewhat mystified.

'That there are two hundred-odd of my bravest and best troops up there in the Vosges Mountains at this very moment. No less an outfit than *Obersturmbannführer* von Dodenburg's SS Assault Regiment Wotan!'

Jodl was impressed. He whistled softly and said, 'Well, sir, if Wotan's up there, organizing the civilians, then it might well work out after all.'

'Of course, it will! Now gentlemen, let us get down to some detailed planning. Time is running out.'

A very happy man now that Germany was going over to the offensive, Adolf Hitler, the Master of the vaunted One Thousand Year Reich, farted yet once again.

CHAPTER 2

Schulze's patrol emerged from the woods as darkness swept across the outskirts of Ste Marie-aux-Mines like a great silent bird. Ahead they could just make out the half-timbered medieval houses, whose chimneys were topped by the empty stork nests typical of Alsace. The locals thought it lucky that the storks returned to the villages each year to bear their young. Here and there thin grey smoke curled up from the high chimneys, but otherwise there was little sign of life. No cow lowed, no child cried, no dog barked. The place might well have been abandoned, but Schulze knew that wasn't so. He told himself that perhaps the *Amis* had imposed a curfew, making the local civilians stay in their houses after dark. Yet somehow he knew that wasn't the answer. After five years of constant combat he had developed a sixth sense which told him when something was wrong. He shivered slightly.

Next to him Matz whispered, 'What's up, old house?'

'Louse ran over my liver,' Schulze answered. 'Come on, it'll be pitch-black soon.' Cautiously, with Schulze and Matz in the lead, clinging to the shadows along the walls, the little patrol stole deeper into the outskirts of Ste Marie – every man wrapped in a cocoon of his own thoughts and assailed by an uneasy sense of vague apprehension. Once one of the troopers rattled his side-arm against the wall and Schulze started as if he had been tweaked with a pair of red-hot pincers. 'Do that agen,' he threatened in a hushed voice, 'and I'll have the frigging eggs off'n you with a razor – a blunt razor!'

Another time a cat suddenly dropped onto the cobbles in front of them, hissing furiously before it fled and leaving them all shaking with nerves.

'Hot steaming shit!' Matz sighed fervently. 'My shitting nerves are going up and down like shitting yo-yos!'

Schulze nodded glumly and concentrated on the task ahead. Hardly daring to breathe, he approached the first tumble-down house – with its smell of animals and boiled white cabbage. As always in France, its windows were tightly shuttered. But somehow Schulze, not normally an emotional or imaginative man, was aware of frightened, apprehensive people inside, waiting expectantly. He halted and wiped his sweating hands on the ragged leg of his trousers. 'Don't like it, Matzi,' he hissed. 'Don't like it one bit.' He tapped the side of his big nose. 'Wooden eye, be on your guard!'

'*Einverstanden*!' Matz whispered, equally apprehensive. 'What's the lark? Even if them civvies inside know we're here, they know we won't harm them; they're as good as our own folks.'

'Exactly. So what's frigging well going on?'

'Well, there's only one way to find out, you big arse-with-ears. Let's go on.'

'Famous last words,' Schulze said mournfully. 'Come on then.' And miserably, nerves jingling electrically, he crept on.

They turned a corner. On the left there was a larger building, with the flags of France and the United States drooping from poles over a doorway bearing the fading legend '*Mairie*' painted on the stonework in blue and white. Telephone wires ran out of the lower window and next to them a stove-pipe poked out. Smoke was coming out of it.

'The townhall,' Schulze whispered. 'Look at them wires – and the pipe. Looks as if that's where the military are.'

Matz gripped his automatic and nodded. 'Do we nobble 'em?'

Schulze hesitated. The C.O. had said that he was only to recce the dump. But what if something alerted the people inside and they began to put up a fight?

'Yer, we'd better,' he hissed. 'Even if there's only some poxed-up frog fart inside there, he could hold off a regiment from behind them walls. Look how frigging thick they are! All right, this is how we're going to do it. Flankers to left . . .'

'And right,' Matz broke in scornfully. 'As soon as they're in position round the back, we go in through the main door.

Christ Almighty, Schulze, d'you think I'm still on my mother's tit? I've been doing this since I was wearing triangular trousers. Come on, let's get on with it!'

But the two old comrades were not destined to assault the town hall – yet. Just as Matz had neatly sliced through the telephone wires with his razor-sharp bayonet, a dark shape detached itself from the wall opposite and hissed, '*Meine Herren!*'

Schulze jerked up his Schmeisser, heart beating furiously, but at the last instant he stopped himself from releasing a swift, vicious burst. 'Christ on a crutch,' he gasped, '*it's a female woman!*'

Matz crossed himself, as if he were in the presence of the Virgin Mary. 'A *real* woman! I didn't know they still had 'em. A real . . . female . . . woman. Oh, catch me, Schulzi, I think I'm going to swoon!' In spite of her fear, Fat Anna giggled.

'*Damn, damn, damn!*' As the fat Alsatian woman, who had appeared so surprisingly out of nowhere, told her tale, von Dodenburg cursed at regular intervals.

'So you see, sir,' Fat Anna concluded, 'they wanted you to make an attack on Ste Marie and then when you attempted to escape, they would trap you up there,' she indicated the faint blur of the ridge on the horizon by raising her hand.

Crouching next to her in the dark square, Schulze felt the soft swish of her big breasts as they rose under the silky material of her blouse and rubbed along his unshaven face. 'Oh,' he groaned to himself, as he felt the old familiar urges in the region of his groin, 'I'd love to put my head between those two and never hear another thing for a couple of weeks!'

Next to him Matz whispered, 'Yer know, Schulze, I could slip her a length o' pork any time she likes, and I wouldn't even charge her ration coupons.'

'Knock it off!' von Dodenburg snapped, irritated beyond measure, as Fat Anna continued her account of the trap being set for Wotan. He thought it was going to be so easy. Now he realized that his weary, hungry young troopers were facing what appeared to be a full battalion of American infantry, complete with tracked vehicles and heavy weapons. What was he to do but beat a hasty retreat before it was too late? Yet, he pondered, as she went on in her guttural Alsatian accent, was there no way that he could not feed his men and still avoid a confrontation with the Americans?

'Some of the new *Amis* have set up their headquarters in the laundry unit camp,' she was saying, again using her arms to indicate its site, her melonlike breasts brushing Schulze's cheek once more, making him clench his teeth with delightful agony.

'What a diamond-cutter I could give her,' he told himself. 'By Christ, I could make her eyes pop with what I've got in my trousers!'

'What did you say, Madame Forstheim?' von Dodenburg snapped, suddenly breaking into her recital.

'Over there, where the *Amis* have their laundry, that's where they are.'

'How many?'

'With the newcomers, there might be a hundred of them at the most,' she answered, wondering a little at the question, and concerned that these young Germans should vanish as quickly as they had appeared. There were too few of them to take Ste Marie-aux-Mines and now, at least, she could let the neighbours know she was a true German patriot and not 'an *Ami* nigger's whore', as they called her behind her back. Hadn't she warned the SS of the trap that had been prepared for them and saved their lives?

Von Dodenburg fell silent. The only sound now was that of the harsh breathing of the young soldiers crouched tensely in the shadows of the church steeple. They waited. Above them the clock started to chime midnight with a harsh, metallic finality.

Von Dodenburg made up his mind. 'Listen,' he announced, as the last stroke boomed, leaving behind a loud echo, 'I'm going to get food for the chaps, come what may. If we are swift, we can get into that . . .'

'Laundry,' Fat Anna prompted him.

'Yes, thanks, laundry in double-quick time. In and out and on our way back to the south and then round the place and into the High Vosges to the north.' He turned to the woman. 'Are you prepared to help us, Madame Forstheim? Remember if you are caught . . .' He left the rest of his sentence unsaid, and frowned hard at her in the poor light.

Fat Anna remembered Louis tumbling and heaving on the bed while she helped 'to pack his laundry', his great naked black bulk, gleaming with sweat, pleading with her to have 'just a little bit more patience . . . he wasn't too well today', and replied firmly, 'When Germany calls, it is the loyal German's duty to answer.'

'Good for you, Madame,' von Dodenburg said.

Next to Schulze, Matz grabbed the front of his pants and moaned, 'Christ, my piece of German salami's calling. Why in three devils' name, ain't she answering? *Oh, I've got a real blue-veiner!*'

But Schulze no longer had time for Matz's sexual privations. Already the C.O. had begun to rap out his orders. There was no time to lose.

Captain Wolf snored contentedly, mouth open, glasses steamed over with the heat coming from the glowing pot-bellied stove in the corner of Louis's office. But the black laundry-commander, try as he may, couldn't get to sleep. His mind was too full of terrible visions of hard-faced blond-haired Germans, armed with frighteningly sharp knives, suddenly seizing him, holding him down, his pants ripped and fallen about his ankles, while one of them, grinning cruelly, prepared to commit the final indignity. Eyes closed, face glazed with sweat, he shuddered violently at the thought – his dong cut off by the grinning mob, just like they did to poor nigger trash down south when those bastard rednecks thought they were getting too sassy. Lawdsakes, why hadn't he stayed in Chicago?

He knew why. Once he had ridden with the Negro Knights of African Freedom – well, not exactly ridden. Dr Givin, the dentist, had ridden on his white charger in front of the parade, carrying a large blue flag and dressed in a blue military uniform. They had marched behind to the rousing Sousa march. How proud he had felt that day! *A Negro Knight of African Freedom*! Then Pearl Harbor had happened and he had volunteered at once, to find that the US Army, anno 1941, was in no particular need of 'Negro Knights of African Freedom'; but they *could* use black laundrymen.

He sighed, eyes still closed. Now, just look where Dr Givin, the dentist, and Sousa's 'Washington Post' had landed him. Here in the middle of nowhere, with a bunch of murderous SS men out there somewhere in the darkness, ready to whip off his meat at the drop of a hat. He shuddered again.

Thirty metres away, Schulze edged himself closer to the sentry supporting himself on his rifle, his helmeted head bowed as if he might well be asleep. In front of him Schulze held his massive right fist, adorned now with what he called the 'Hamburg equalizer', a set of fearsome brass knuckles that had done yeoman service in the waterfront brawls of his youth. He knew that silence was essential. 'Hit them, choke them, *bite* them if you like,' von Dodenburg had commanded, 'but no shooting. At all costs we mustn't alarm all the *amis* up in the hills!'

Now Schulze was within striking distance of the sentry. He drew a careful breath and brought up his brass-shod fist. It was now or never. Suddenly, to his horror, the sentry began to stir. He made strange choking noises like men do when they are waking from a shallow sleep. The bastard was coming to! Schulze hesitated no longer. With surprising speed for such a big man, he sprang forward. He caught a glimpse of a frightened black face – all gleaming white teeth and rolling yellow eyes. Then he lunged. Next instant he howled with pain, as his brass knuckles struck the sentry's helmet.

'*Himmel, Arsch und Wolken . . .*' Schulze's curse ended in a gasp for air, as the negro reacted with surprising speed. The butt of his rifle slammed into Schulze's belly. He reeled back against the wall at the same instant that his opponent dropped his rifle and whipped something out of his pocket.

Schulze gasped with horror as he caught a faint glimpse of steel in the poor light. The negro had pulled out a cut-throat razor and it was clear that he was intending to use it.

'I'm gonna carve you, brother,' the negro crooned and next moment he lashed out. Schulze ducked swiftly and threw an ineffective punch at the other man. The negro chuckled softly, as if he were enjoying this little battle in the middle of the night in the supposedly deserted courtyard. 'You're gonna lack a set o' ears, dude,' he chortled. 'Now get this.'

'*Shit, Schulze!*' Matz cried, 'without me you're frigging helpless.' He hit the back of the negro's neck with a sock filled with sand. '*Frigging, absolutely helpless!*'

The negro gave a soft groan and pitched forward straight into Schulze's arms, the razor clattering from his nerveless fingers to the ground.

Inside the office Second-Lieutenant Louis heard the faint noise and the whispered conversation. Instinctively he knew what was happening. He closed his eyes even more firmly and began to pray, the sweat streaming down his contorted black face in rivulets. 'Spare my meat, Lawd,' he prayed. '*Oh, please spare ma meat!*'

CHAPTER 3

Controlled chaos reigned. Everywhere the happy Wotan troopers scurried back and forth, grabbing food and drink, stuffing their packs with Hershey bars and cartons of Lucky Strike, excited grins on their unshaven faces, like schoolboys who had just been let loose on the tuck-shop.

Happily swigging can after can of Schlitz beer while he supervised the looting of the laundry unit, Schulze proclaimed to no one in particular (for Matz had unaccountably disappeared), 'On pay nights my old man used to take out his false teeth and play *Deutschland uber Alles* on them with a kitchen spoon. Now what do you say to that, comrades?'

But Schulze's 'comrades' were too busy stuffing their pockets with loot to be concerned with Herr Schulze Senior's musical talents.

Inside the office von Dodenburg gave a weary grin as he heard Schulze's voice and concentrated again on the interrogation of his two prisoners. Time was running out fast and he wanted to find out as much as he could before they took to the mountains.

'Right then,' he barked, all arrogant, SS officer, 'my informant tells me that you have a battalion of troops located outside the town. Where is it *exactly*?'

Wolf, who spoke German perfectly, shrugged, apparently unconcerned by the naked threat revealed in von Dodenburg's lean hard face, and said casually, '*Nix versteh.*'

Next to him Louis wrung his hands, the beads of perspiration showering from his fat face, and pleaded, 'Don't do it, Cap'n, suh. Please don't cut off my meat. *Please!*' He knelt with difficulty and raised his hands in the classic pose of supplication.

Von Dodenburg managed to keep a stern face only with difficulty. The fat negro was such a pathetic coward that he was almost comic. He repeated his request more slowly in his laboured English and indicated the map on the wall with a jerk of his automatic. 'Show me on that, *quick*!'

Louis did not need a second invitation. He stumbled to his feet and waddled across to the map hurriedly. Wolf shook his head in despair. Poor frightened Louis was going to spoil everything. All the same he could not but admire the SS Colonel. He seemed to epitomize the arrogance and boldness of the SS, with his hard face and aggressive blue eyes; even the old scar which ran the length of his cheek fitted in perfectly with the tough image. If there were many more Colonels of SS in the *Wehrmacht* like this one, he told himself grimly, it was still going to be a damned long war.

Von Dodenburg, standing by the map under the yellow light of the naked electric bulb, took in the information that poured from Louis's thick lips, one ear listening to the sounds outside, waiting for the first unusual one that would indicate that the other *Amis* had been alerted to what was happening in the laundry unit. Somewhere there was a strange creaking like that made by rusty bed springs, but he dismissed it. Finally Louis dried up, stumbling to a halt, hands falling to the base of his stomach, as if he were still afraid for his 'meat'. His eyes were glued frantically to the young German's harsh face, seeking some clue to his fate.

Von Dodenburg's mind raced. Now that he knew the enemy's dispositions around Ste Marie-aux-Mines, he knew that it would be terribly difficult for his weary men to make it into the mountains without being discovered. The slightest thing could alarm the waiting *Amis* and they had vehicles. 'I need wheels,' he told himself, while the negro stared at him fearfully, hands still clutching his groin. He spun round on the white man, who had the look of a Jew about him, and snapped, 'You, Captain, how many trucks do you have here?'

Wolf shot Louis a warning look. 'Only a couple, Colonel,' he answered, 'and they are all shot – not in working order,' he added quickly when he saw that the SS officer did not understand the word 'shot'.

'Is that true?' von Dodenburg barked at Louis, knowing instinctively that cunning-looking Captain was lying.

'Nosuh,' Louis replied promptly. 'We've got about six deuces-and-a-half.'

Wolf groaned inwardly and stopped listening. Louis had well and truly fucked things up.

When Sergeant-Major Schulze took to the drink, even when it was merely weak American beer, which he characterized scornfully as 'gnats' piss', his thoughts invariably turned to the pleasures of the flesh, or as he would express it in his honest, direct fashion, '*hot, steaming female gash*'.

As the troopers dashed back and forth, looting the American unit, their prisoners lined up against the wall, flanked by machine guns, Schulze suddenly remembered the fat Alsatian woman who had led them to this place. *Where was Fat Anna?* He bolted down the rest of his beer, tossed the can to one of the black prisoners – who caught it instinctively – scratched his loins and bellowed to the nearest sergeant, 'Take charge, plush-ears. I'm off on a mission.' With that he turned and strode towards the huts, wondering which one housed Fat Anna and her ample charms.

As he walked, he sang softly to himself, anticipating the juicy pleasures to come:

> 'I don't want a bayonet up my asshole,
> I don't want my bollocks shot away,
> I'd rather live in Germany,
> In merry, merry Germany.
> *And fornicate my fuckin' life away.*

Highly pleased with himself, Schulze stopped suddenly. His ears had taken in a familiar sound – the rhythmic squeaking of bed springs. 'Like a frigging fiddler's elbow!' he breathed in awe. 'By the Great Whore of Buxtehude,' he roared, 'where the hounds piss outa their elbows, who's porking around here – *without my permission*?' He paused, hands on his hips, and glared suspiciously at the blacked-out huts, trying to ascertain the source of that frustratingly delightful mattress-music.

Then he had it – the hut next to the fat nigger's office. There was no mistaking it. That's where it was coming from. Face crimson with rage at this insult, Schulze lumbered into a run, mumbling, 'The nerve, the frigging nerve. Cocking his leg over, while his senior sergeant has a diamond-cutter right up to his chin and not a diamond in sight!'

He fumbled with the door of the hut. There was no mistaking what was going on inside the place. The moans of joy and harsh gasps for breath made it all too clear. He turned the knob. The damned place was locked and inside they were going at it like a couple of race horses charging down the final stretch. Schulze grunted with rage and, stumbling back a few paces, charged. He hit the door with his right shoulder. It splintered. With a loud crack the lock snapped and suddenly he was stumbling inside to stop abruptly, a look of absolute awe on his face. Like a naked yellow monkey with one leg, that familiar figure was energetically pumping at Fat Anna, naked too, a mass of heavy fleshy hips and enormous breasts that almost engulfed the one-legged monkey so that he looked almost as if he were ascending a fleshy Everest.

For one moment, he stood, unable to believe the evidence of his own bulging eyes, shocked into open-mouthed gaping silence, while the two of them, oblivious of the observer, continued their mad gallop, all bouncing flesh and gasping breath. Then he found his voice. He let out a tremendous bellow that made the very walls of the place tremble. '*Matz*!' he cried, '*will you get your filthy porker outa that lady – at frigging once!*'

Wolf didn't hesitate as the SS Colonel, startled by the sudden yell, spun round. With surprising agility for such an unhealthy-looking man, he dived forward. With one hand he ripped the blackout curtain from the window at the rear of

the office. With the other he whipped open the catch. Next
minute he had thrown himself through it, dropped on his feet
and was running rapidly into the darkness, arms working like
pistons, head ducked deep down between his skinny shoulders.

Von Dodenburg raised his Schmeisser, and then he let the
weapon sink again. He hadn't a chance in hell of hitting the
man – who had almost vanished into the night now. Besides,
he didn't want to alarm the *Amis* in the hills above Ste Marie.
They'd hear soon enough what was going on in the laundry
depot. Instead he swung round and shouted at the terrified
negro, 'Now listen, if you value your life and those of your
men, do *exactly* what I order from now on. Do you
understand?'

'Yessir, cap'n, I understand,' Louis quavered, trembling
with fear.

'Right, then, move it!' Louis moved it.

Von Dodenburg sprang into action, realizing that every
minute was precious. Swiftly he organized the convoy,
allotting a prisoner to each truck, next to a Wotan driver,
perching another couple on the open deck behind. He knew
that what he was doing was contrary to the Geneva
Convention, but as a cynical voice at the back of his head
sneered, 'Christ, they're gonna shoot you as a war criminal
anyway, if you survive. *So what?*' 'So what indeed,' he said to
himself as he dashed back and forth, constantly throwing
worried glances at the dark range of hills above Ste Marie.
But for the time being they remained silent. So far the little
Jew who had escaped had evidently not reached the men dug
in up there. But von Dodenburg knew that he would – all too
soon. He harboured no illusions about that.

The convoy began to form up and the happy looks began to
vanish from the faces of his young men, as they stowed the
looted goodies about their persons and checked their weapons
for the battle to come. Even the most callow and carefree of
them knew what danger they were in as long as they
remained in Ste Marie.

Von Dodenburg dug Louis in the ribs. 'All right,

Lieutenant,' he commanded. 'Up in the first truck.'

'Me sah?'

'Yes, you, sah!' von Dodenburg mimicked his accent maliciously, wondering what kind of a war it was in which the *Amis* hoped that their oppressed black minority would fight for them with any conviction. It was like asking the Poles to do battle for National Socialist Germany.

His face green with fear, Louis clambered ponderously onto the truck, mumbling something about being a member of 'garment workers' union' and 'a non-combatant'.

In spite of the urgency of the moment, von Dodenburg grinned at the reluctant black man. Soon he was going to learn that a bullet took no heed of whether a man was a union man and a non-combatant or not. A slug, just like a male erection, knew no morality whatsoever.

'All right, you bunch of cardboard soldiers,' he called, checking up and down the column, seeing if everything was ready for the move, 'prepare to move out . . .'

Suddenly he stopped, aware that something was wrong. Where were Schulze and his running-mate Corporal Matz? 'Anyone seen Sergeant Schulze?' he called. There were a few muted catcalls and whistles. Someone cried, 'If I know anything about him, sir, he'll be somewhere with his snout in the trough or the sauce bottle!'

Von Dodenburg nodded. That would be it. The pair of rogues would have found something stronger than the weak American beer that the others had been drinking. He cupped his hands around his mouth and called, 'Schulze! Where are you Schulze? Come on, man, at the double now.'

The rest of his words were drowned by a sudden soft plop, followed immediately by the obscene howl of a mortar bomb hurtling through the night sky.

'Incoming mail!' someone yelled in sudden alarm.

Von Dodenburg spun round. On the horizon small spurts of cherry-red flame had erupted everywhere. With a sinking feeling he knew that the little Jew had reached his own people. *The Amis knew they were here!*

He wasted no more time. He waved his arm urgently. '*Roll 'em!*' he cried as the first mortar bomb exploded with an ugly crump a hundred metres away. '*Get those trucks moving, drivers!*' *ROLL 'EM!*

Everywhere the drivers started their engines. The little courtyard erupted with noise. The night air was filled with the stench of gasoline. Suddenly all was noise and hectic activity. In the backs of the trucks the young troopers fumbled with their weapons, knowing that they had a fight on their hands. The black soldiers cowered with fear and, in the lead truck, Second Lieutenant Louis began to pray, in between cursing Dr Givin, the dentist, and his damned 'Negro Knights of African Freedom'.

Von Dodenburg waited, Schmeisser unslung and cocked, ready for action; and there they were, the two rogues, Schulze cursing and raging, with Matz hopping beside him, trying to strap on his wooden leg. While behind them waddled the fat Alsatian woman, naked as the day she was born, weeping miserably and, at the same time, blowing kisses at a departing Matz.

Von Dodenburg groaned and then they were off, as, above them, the horizon erupted in flames.

CHAPTER 4

The trucks were rolling at full speed through an alarmed Ste Marie. On all sides there came frantic cries in German, French, English. Tracer slashed the darkness violently. Officers bellowed orders. NCOs blew their whistles. Up front in the cab with Louis, while Matz and Schulze perched on the roof, von Dodenburg cast anxious glances to left and right as they roared through narrow cobbled streets. It only took one truck to be knocked out and the whole convoy would be stalled.

Next to him the terrified Louis mopped his brow while the young driver crashed through his gears as they began the steep ascent that led out of the grim little mining town. Von Dodenburg reached up and slapped the roof of the cab. 'Keep your eyes peeled, Schulze,' he bellowed above the roar of the engine. 'This is probably where they'll try it.'

'Peeled like a tin of tomatoes!' Schulze roared back, in high good humour once more at the prospect of violent action.

They were labouring up the slope in second gear, the trucks losing their convoy distance, crowding together and making an even better target von Dodenburg couldn't help thinking, for any Americans waiting for them up there in the pass.

A sudden burst of slugs and the windscreen in front of them shattered into a glittering spider's web. Louis screamed hysterically, like a woman. Next to him the driver reeled back, his face looking as if someone had thrown a handful of strawberry jam at it. Von Dodenburg grabbed the wheel with one hand. With the other he kept the dying youngster's leg pressed down firmly on the accelerator.

'Knock the glass clear,' he yelled at Louis. 'Quick, or I'll shoot you myself! *Move it*!'

The threat worked. The fat lieutenant seized a spanner from the glove compartment and started knocking out the shattered glass, while von Dodenburg steered by instinct. A blast of icy night air struck him in the face. Now he could see the road once more. He gasped with relief, though it wasn't a very encouraging prospect.

There were stabs of angry scarlet flame cutting the darkness on both sides. The *Amis* were in position in force in the fir trees which lined the steep winding road. Above him Matz and Schulze took up the challenge. Veterans that they were, they snapped off short controlled bursts to left and right, forcing the Americans to keep low.

A bright red bolt of fire shot towards them, trailing fiery sparks behind it. Von Dodenburg ducked instinctively. It hissed by the truck and exploded harmlessly on the other side of the road. '*Bazooka bastards*!' he heard Schulze bellow above the roar of the engine as he fired a sharp burst into the trees. An *Ami* fell, all flailing arms, and that was the end of the bazooka fire. But there were other dangers to come.

As they turned a bend in the winding road, von Dodenburg's heart sank. There was no mistaking that silhouette. An American Sherman tank was rolling out of the trees, churning its way up the embankment on to the road, its tracks churning up the mud.

Louis threw up his fat hands. 'Colonel, suh, that's a tank!' he cried in horror. 'Coming straight at us, Colonel, sir. What are we gonna do?'

'*This*!' von Dodenburg hissed through gritted teeth, as the Sherman rolled to a stop on the side of the road, the electrically operated turret hissing round, bringing its long gun to bear on the convoy. He pressed the dead man's foot down on the accelerator – *hard*!

The truck leapt forward. 'Hold on up there!' von Dodenburg cried to the men on the cab, carried away by the unreasoning excitement of combat. Above, Schulze and Matz answered with a burst of fire at the Sherman's turret, the tracer hissing towards it like a flight of angry hornets.

Von Dodenburg tensed as the Sherman shuddered. Then scarlet flame stabbed the darkness and the truck rocked frighteningly, as if struck by a tornado, as the great shell whizzed by. It exploded fifty metres beyond, showering the convoy with clods of earth and gravel. Now they were only metres apart. Von Dodenburg prepared to take the shock, his face contorted like that of a madman. Louis sat back glued to his seat, his yellow eyes threatening to pop out of their sockets at any moment. 'Lawd save me!' he moaned, 'Oh, please Lawd save me!'

With a rending, metallic howl, the two vehicles collided. Von Dodenburg felt his head slam against a stanchion. For a moment he blacked out. When he came to, head ringing, bright red stars were exploding before his eyes. He shook his head and things came back into focus. To his front, leather-helmeted American tankers were frantically trying to escape from the stalled Sherman, while tracer bounced off its armour like smoking golf-balls. The front of the truck was crumpled like a metallic banana skin. Smoke poured thickly from the ruptured engine. And all the time intense enemy fire came from the trees on both sides.

Von Dodenburg shook his head again and realized he must act and act immediately. Behind the wrecked truck, the others were beginning to slow down to a walk. His men were sitting ducks inside them. He had to get them moving again.

'Get out!' he cried in sudden rage at Louis, who was bleeding heavily from a great gash in the side of his face. 'Get out, man!' Enfuriated, he pushed the fat negro who almost fell out of the cab. Von Dodenburg followed and waved his arms furiously at the driver of the next truck. '*Roll 'em!*' he cried over the angry snap-and-crackle of the small arms battle raging everywhere.

The driver accelerated at the same instant that Matz and Schulze dropped to the road, Schmeissers blazing at their hips. The first of the Americans, rushing out of the woods, reeled back, screaming and crying out in mortal agony as they ran straight into that deadly burst of fire.

Von Dodenburg grabbed hold of the dazed Louis. 'Listen

you, you're gonna get us out of here or it's going to cost your black hide!' he yelled above the noise.

'Get you out?' Louis repeated helplessly, quaking with fear. 'How, sir?'

Von Dodenburg didn't answer him, but yelled to the driver of the second truck, edging his way past the wrecked vehicle, 'Turf out the *Amis*! At the double, you drivers! Get the negroes out, under guard! *Los, los, los!*'

Next to him Schulze grinned as he went on firing. 'The Old Man's got it, Matzi,' he yelled. 'He's gonna screw them *Amis* after all!'

'What do you mean, you big-horned ox?' Matz cried, but Schulze had no time to answer. The black Americans in the woods were rallying and coming out into the open once more. He spun his Schmeisser from left to right, hosing them down, trying to give his C.O. a chance to carry out his plan, the only way to save what was left of Wotan.

'You, Louis!' von Dodenburg cried above the racket, 'get your men organized. At the double now.' He pushed the bewildered Louis towards his laundry workers who were being kicked and shoved out of the stalled trucks.

'Organized?' Louis quavered, his face a strange green colour in the unnatural light of the flares which were dropping on all sides.

'Yes,' von Dodenburg yelled in exasperation. 'In two columns on both sides of the trucks. Quick now!' He nodded to Schulze. 'Get him moving, for God's sake, Schulze!'

Schulze grinned and dug the muzzle of his Schmeisser into Louis's trembling flesh. 'Move it, arse-with-ears. You heard what the C.O. said. *LOS!*'

The fat lieutenant might not have understood the German, but he understood that hard metal pressing into his ribs all right. He began to call his laundry boys together.

Petersen and his staff, crouching near the top of the pass, could see the Germans quite clearly now, silhouetted as they were in the garish light of the flares, while tracer bullets zipped back and forth in a lethal glowing morse. In spite of the fire, the Germans were moving once more, their trucks crawling up the ascent at a snail's pace.

Just behind Petersen, Master-Sergeant Lee gripped his grease gun more tightly in hands which were damp with sweat. Nevertheless he felt quite cool. This was the first time that 'Petersen's Fighting Coons' had gone into action – and against white men at that. But he knew they were as calm and collected as he was. Their first volley had been ragged, but now they had settled down. The Krauts were going to get their asses kicked. They'd never make it to the top of the pass. They simply *couldn't* make it.

Lee waited tensely for Colonel Petersen to give the order to the men waiting on both sides to open fire with all they had. The Krauts would be wiped off the face of the earth when he did. *But what was taking the Old Man so long?*

Colonel Petersen and Wolf continued to stare through their night glasses at the slowly advancing Germans, as yet another flare exploded above the line of trucks, outlining them perfectly in its icy light. Then Wolf lowered his glasses and broke the brooding silence. 'Sir,' he gasped, 'you've got five minutes at the most. Then they'll be over the pass. They'll have made it.'

Almost sadly Petersen lowered his glasses at last. When he spoke, his voice was low and weary. 'But don't you see, Wolf, what the Kraut bastards have done? They're using those helpless laundry boys as a human shield. If I order my men to open fire, we'll kill our own people. Goddammit, it's against all the rules of Land Warfare to do a thing like that!'

Wolf laughed hollowly. 'Since when have the SS respected the Rules of Land Warfare, sir? But you can't let them get away just like that. Army HQ is desperate to know what these SS joes are up to in the Vosges. If they make their escape now, all hell will be let loose at Higher Headquarters. Sir,' he choked desperately. 'They'll be screaming out for heads, *your head*! Think of your career!'

Petersen looked at him squarely, as if he were seeing him for the first time. 'They can have it, Captain. Especially if they think I'm going to fire at my own people. There'll be another time, I promise you,' he added grimly, as the first of the trucks began to bridge the rise.

'*My own people!*' Master-Sergeant Lee repeated the words as if they were holy. For a moment the escaping Krauts were forgotten as he savoured those three simple words the Old Man had said; '*My own people!*'

At that moment, he knew he would gladly die for Colonel Oscar Petersen, a white man who thought of the blacks as his 'own people'.

Below them the SS trucks began to disappear into the darkness without a single shot being fired at them. Wotan had done it again. Standing up in the lead truck, a jubilant Schulze raised his right leg and ripped off a tremendous fart of triumph, crying at the dug-in Americans, 'Assholes up! *Three cheers for America*!' And then he fell against Matz, giggling like an excited schoolgirl.

CHAPTER 5

The bitter wind had dropped and it was a little warmer, but the afternoon sky had changed dramatically. The sharp blue had become a leaden grey. At the head of the long column spread out along the ridge – they had abandoned the captured American trucks at dawn – von Dodenburg sniffed the air like a dog trying to pick up a scent. He frowned.

To his right, Schulze also frowned. He knew what the C.O. was thinking, 'Snow, sir?' he asked, though he knew the answer already.

Von Dodenburg, his face tense and strained, nodded. 'Yes, the sky's full of violins,' he answered using the old soldier's slang.

Schulze groaned. 'That'll really put the tick-tock in the old pisspot! Those wettails of ours,' he glanced back at the young Wotan troopers, 'are bushed as it is. The snow'll fuck 'em up for good.'

Von Dodenburg nodded. 'But it might put off the *Ami Jabos**. You can bet your life they are out searching for us at this very moment.' He glanced at the sombre grey sky, as if one of the feared fighter-bombers might come roaring in, cannon chattering, at any moment.

'Suppose you're right, sir. But snow . . .' Schulze shivered and hitched up the two rifles, taken from weary troopers, which he was carrying in addition to his own Schmeisser, and said no more. Like every one else in that weary band of fugitives, he concentrated on simply moving.

Von Dodenburg forced the pace as they climbed higher and higher, skinny chests heaving with the effort. The icy mountain air stabbed their lungs like a sharp knife with every breath. Icicles began to form on their beards and glitter silver-white in their eyebrows. Like old men, they toiled

* Fighter-bombers

upwards, staggering, slipping, falling on the rough frozen ground. But von Dodenburg showed no mercy. He knew that to stop now would be fatal.

Here and there a young trooper would fall on all fours. When pleading didn't help, a harsh-faced von Dodenburg would draw his pistol and cry above the man's choking efforts to regain his breath: 'Up, man . . . or I'll shoot you like a dog where you lie. *UP!*'

The threat always worked. Somehow or other the trooper would struggle to his feet and carry on, swaying and staggering like a drunk.

Hour after hour the torture continued, with von Dodenburg snarling over and over again, 'March you dogs . . . *march or die!*' And they marched on, chests heaving, breath coming in strangled gasps, sweat pouring down their ashen faces, eyes blind to everything but the next few metres. And all the while the sky above them grew greyer. It wouldn't be long now before the storm started.

'When the frig are we gonna stop running, sir?' Schulze gasped.

'*Withdrawing* please, Schulze.' Von Dodenburg tried to appease the scarlet-faced NCO. But Schulze didn't seem to hear. 'We've been on the frigging run ever since May back in macaroni-land when the Tommies chased us out of Monte Cassino. All the way through frigging France, and now here.' He spat in disgust. 'When's it gonna stop, sir? I can tell you this for straight, Frau Schulze's handsome son has had a frigging 'nough of all this running. He wants to go home to mother.'

Von Dodenburg wiped the sweat from his forehead. 'I know, Schulze, I know. We've all had enough. Battle after battle. Run and fight and then run again. My God, when the Vulture* took us into Italy, Wotan was three thousand strong. Look at us now – a pathetic handful of survivors.' He stared at the sky, as if appealing to God himself to have mercy

* See *Guns at Cassino* for further details

on them. But that day God was looking the other way.

Schulze caught the look of concern on the C.O.'s face and regretted that he had ever spoken. He forced a grin. 'Don't worry, sir. After this, it'll be roses, roses all the frigging way.'

'Roses all the frigging way!' von Dodenburg echoed the words and forced a weary grin. 'Of course, it will be, you big rogue.'

'Yes sir,' Schulze said, hitching up the rifles to a more comfortable position on his shoulder, 'I think after this I'll retire from the SS. Let some ambitious young man like Corporal Matz take over my high position.' Matz muttered a weary obscenity.

Schulze ignored it. 'What I'll probably do is retire to Hamburg and become a kept man. I mean what I've got in my pants is worth a fortune – and I've been giving it away all the time. Women have allus been crazy for my alabaster torso and I've been *meschugge* enough to have given it away. What a generous, crazy fool I am,' he added modestly.

Matz groaned and made a motion as if he were pulling a lavatory chain. But Schulze didn't seem to notice. Instead he frowned as if he were seriously considering the proposition. 'Probably some titled woman would be my collar-size. Not the poor aristocracy, mind you,' he added, 'but one of that lot with a castle and plenty of marie*. I mean, I've got to keep up me standards. There's my lung torpedoes to be bought, and of course, my suds. And . . .'

'*Silence*!' von Dodenburg rasped, flinging up his arm to cut off Schulze's flow of words. He shot a look to the east, ears straining to catch the slightest sound. Around him the column staggered to a halt, the young troopers too exhausted to care. They simply stood there, shoulders bent as if in defeat, skinny young bodies racked with pain.

'Look!' von Dodenburg hissed. 'Three o'clock!'

There was a soft rumble, a glint like a speck of mica. The little *Luftwaffe* sergeant gasped. '*Jabo, Ami Jabo!*'

* Army slang for money

Von Dodenburg reacted immediately. 'Into the trees; both sides of the trail!' he yelled.

There were two of them, barrel-engines roaring, zipping along at tree-top height, their silver bodies gleaming.

'*Ami Thunderbolts*!' the *Luftwaffe* pilot began; then he was crushed by the body of a Wotan trooper falling on top of him.

Von Dodenburg tensed. The *Amis* had spotted them, he knew that. Soon they would come in for the kill, and the trees offered little protection. He waited for the inevitable.

Suddenly the leader waggled his wings. Von Dodenburg's heart sank to his boots. *They had been seen!*

'Ready for trouble, men!' he cried above the roar of the engines. 'They know we're here. *Here they come . . .*'

The rest of his words were drowned by the sound of a thousand whips. Scarlet flame crackled the length of the leading plane's wing. The sky was filled with the snarl of engines, the hiss of tracer fire, the stench of fuel oil and cordite, as all around the quavering troopers the pine needles came tumbling down in a furious green rain. With an ear-splitting roar the two Thunderbolts raced above them, dragging their evil shadows behind them. Von Dodenburg caught a glimpse of the white stars and stripes of the Invasion army on their wings, and then they were gone, hurtling effortlessly into the grey sky.

With a sinking feeling, von Dodenburg knew what the pilots were attempting to do. Even if they couldn't kill the men on the ground below, they *could* pin them down until the follow-up infantry caught up with them, and this time, the handsome young Colonel realized, Wotan was not going to escape. If they couldn't deal with the enemy *jabos* soon, Wotan would be finished.

Four miles away Colonel Petersen smiled as he heard the muted rat-tat-tat of the Thunderbolts' machine guns, and beamed in spite of the strain. The flyboys had located the Kraut SS at last. 'Did you hear that, Captain?'

Wolf returned the Colonel's smile. In spite of his weedy

physique, the skinny little Intelligence Captain was standing the pace as well as Petersen's much younger infantrymen. 'It's coming from over there, sir, to the north-west!'

Behind them, Master-Sergeant Lee's radio crackled into action. The signaller held up the phone for the NCO. Hastily he snatched it and listened to what the unknown soldier at the other end had to say before exclaiming, 'Colonel, sir, the Krauts have gotten their asses in a sling! Begging your pardon, sir,' he pulled himself together with an effort, black face glistening with sweat but wreathed in a big smile. 'That was the flyboys' air-ground controller. They've located the SS and pinned them down. Map co-ordinate . . .'

Colonel Petersen whipped out his map and marked the spot on it with his chinagraph pencil, his face as excited as the NCO's. Then he looked up and cried, his breath fogging grey on the icy air, 'All right, you men, what are you waiting for?'

Lee took up the cry. 'All right, guys, let's move out. We've got the Krauts!'

Their black faces beamed at the news. '*They've got the Krauts!*' The words flew from man to man. Suddenly their weary young bodies were enthused with new energy and the adrenalin began pumping. In a flash all weariness had vanished.

Petersen waited no longer. He settled his carbine more comfortably on his shoulder and cried, 'Follow me!'

Next to him Captain Wolf said a quick prayer that this time Petersen's 'Fighting Coons' would pull it off. This time his young black men deserved success.

'*And the frigging landlady also blows the frigging trombone!*' Schulze said obscurely, as the Thunderbolts came round in a slow tight curve, ready for a new attack, both of them lowering their undercarriages as they did so. That would act as an effective air brake, cutting down their speed considerably. 'The bastards are coming in for the kill!' he yelled above the roar of their radial engines.

Von Dodenburg, crouching at the roadside, sought desperately for some way out of the trap in which they found themselves. But as the sinister silver birds came lower and lower, he knew there was none. If only it would snow, he moaned to himself. That would give them the cover they needed so desperately. But the snow refused to come. Von Dodenburg clenched his fists angrily and waited.

The leading Thunderbolt filled the sky ahead. The firs whipped back and forth with its prop wash. Von Dodenburg could see the pale blur of the pilot's face behind the glass. This time the bastard couldn't miss. He tensed, hugging the ground like a passionate lover.

Suddenly the Thunderbird shuddered. For an instant it seemed to stop dead, as if it had run into an invisible wall. Shrieking like crazy banshees, two rockets streaked towards the men cowering on the ground, trailing parallel lines of white smoke behind them. But the pilot had fired a little too early. The rockets howled above them and slammed into the forest two hundred metres behind. Firs snapped and tumbled like matchwood. The blast slapped their faces like a wet fist. The very breath was snatched from their lungs, leaving them gasping and choking like asthmatics in the throes of an attack. Then the Thunderbolt howled above their heads and soared effortlessly into the sky.

Schulze gave a great howl of rage. He stumbled to his feet and grabbed hold of the heavy MG 42 as if it were a child's toy. 'Matz,' he yelled above the roar of the second plane, 'on your frigging knees. *At the double now, ape turd!*'

Matz understood immediately. He dropped on his knees in the middle of the track and tensed. Schulze didn't hesitate. He flung the machine gun over the little corporal's back and aimed, a red-faced David facing up to a metallic and lethal Goliath.

The second plane advanced at them with frightening slowness, the roar of its engine seeming to fill the whole world with crazy, ear-splitting noise. Von Dodenburg prayed. He prayed like he had never prayed in his life before. Schulze, for his part, cursed, cursed and cursed, as the Thunderbolt filled his sights. He could see every rivet, the dark stains where the oil had leaked on to the metal, the 'burns' on the rubber of the wheels. 'Come to baby, come to baby,' he pleaded, finger curled, white-knuckled, round the trigger of the machine gun.

The Thunderbolt pilot opened up and tongues of flame rippled the length of the wings. Burning white tracer sped towards the lone gunner, racing towards him with ever-increasing speed. Schulze held his ground, face set and grim. The slugs ripped up the trail in angry little spurts. Still Schulze did not open fire. Von Dodenburg groaned and clenched sweat-drenched fists in rage and despair.

Then Schulze's shoulder went rigid and the machine gun erupted into violent life. The belt raced through the chamber. The air was full of the stink of burned cordite. Gleaming brass cartridges clattered to the ground next to Matz's head. At that range Schulze couldn't miss.

Things began to happen to the Thunderbolt. Bright silver shards of metal flew from its ripped fuselage. Its shattered engine coughed. The prop went dead. Glycol streamed up from it and covered the cockpit in white blinding fury. Von Dodenburg caught one last glimpse of the horrified pilot throwing up both hands in terror and then the plane was sailing over their heads completely out of control. Schulze let go of the machine gun. Matz collapsed on the cartridge-littered trail, gasping for breath as if he had just run a great race.

The stricken plane hit the top of the pines which were sheered off instantly. Some snapped like matchwood, but they did the trick. One of the plane's wings was ripped off like a metal leaf as it reeled to one side and hit the ground. There was a thunderous roar. In a great ball of blinding smoke, tinged with cherry-red flame, its gas tank exploded. A moment later it had disappeared and a mushroom of smoke started to rise into the leaden sky.

'*Hurrah! Hurrah!*' The troopers began to cheer, but at that very same instant the dead pilot's colleague was over them again, spraying the area with bursts of machine-gun fire, the slugs whizzing towards them like a flight of vicious red hornets. Desperately they hugged the ground as the bullets cut the trees all about them. Then the plane sailed high into the air, not risking the same fate as had overtaken its fellow.

Von Dodenburg realized immediately what the second American was trying to do. He would pin them down with the occasional burst of machine-gun fire, keeping well out of Schulze's range, trapping them thus until the ground troops arrived. Schulze's victory had been short-lived. He knew it, too, for suddenly he cried out in frustration, '*The bastard! He's still got us bogged down with our hooters in the crap! Hell's bells, won't Wotan ever get frigging lucky?*'

But for once SS Assault Regiment Wotan *was* going to be lucky. Crouching there as he tried to think of some way out of the trap they were in, von Dodenburg felt a sudden wetness on his cheek. Puzzled, he looked up and grinned. A snowflake was dancing lazily in front of him, and it wasn't alone. There were more of the delightful little creatures, and they were getting thicker by the minute. '*Snow!*' he bellowed, new hope surging through his emaciated body, '*It's beginning to snow!*'

The excited cry was taken up on all sides, as the sky grew darker by the instant and the noise of the lone plane began to die away.

Von Dodenburg sprang to his feet, careless of any danger now, knowing that they had to take full advantage of the snow storm. 'On your feet!' he yelled. 'Move out. *Los jetzt, vorwarts!*'

The excited troopers stumbled to their feet, like schoolboys released from the classroom. Hastily they formed up, careless of the plane circling above them somewhere in the storm. Von Dodenburg rapped out his orders and with the snow already settling on their helmets, they set off once again on their long journey to Schloss Falkenstein. Five minutes later they had disappeared, the snow soon obliterating all signs of their passing.

CHAPTER 6

The long climb was hellish. In grim silence, broken only by the sound of their own laboured breathing, the young troopers slogged up the snow-bound trail, the snowflakes whirling all about them. The storm, which had been such a blessing, now became a curse. The wind racing across the mountains lashed the snow into their strained faces, slashing at them like a myriad razors. The icy air stabbed their lungs. Their boots were transformed into clumsy balls of hard-pressed snow. Like old men, they trailed ever higher, staggering, falling and slipping on the slick surface of the snowfield.

But von Dodenburg allowed them no respite. They had to find Schloss Falkenstein and get under cover before the storm abated, for he knew their pursuers would send in their planes as soon as the snow stopped, and they wouldn't escape the enemy *jabos* a second time.

As always, Schulze was a pillar of strength. In spite of his own craving for respite from the burning agony of this terrible march, he paced up and down the long, strung-out column, threatening, pleading, cajoling, even occasionally striking the weary young troopers to keep them going, crying in feigned rage, 'By the Great God and all His Triangles, if you don't move that lazy ass of yours, I'll stick my bayonet up it – *sideways*!' And that terrible threat always worked. Somehow the trooper managed to carry on.

In spite of his own overwhelming weariness, von Dodenburg felt a dull warming glow inside. He knew the *Amis*. Not that he discounted them in the manner of many SS officers, dismissing them as third-rate soldiers, who could only win if they were supported by planes and an overwhelming artillery bombardment. But he *did* know that their infantrymen were not capable of the sheer hard slog that the SS were used to. Mostly, if the Americans did not have their precious 'wheels', they were lost; and in these mountains 'wheels' would be of no use. So, confident that American ground troops could not follow them up here in the High Vosges, von Dodenburg slogged on through the storm, seeking the mysterious castle mentioned in Himmler's orders, constantly referring to the compass strapped to his wrist; for now visibility was down to less than fifty metres. 'A real old soup-kitchen,' Schulze had commented and he was right. Von Dodenburg had to keep his eye on the flickering green needle of the wrist compass all the time, taking a fix at five minute intervals and checking his position with his map. If he went wrong in these mountains under present conditions, that would be the end of Wotan.

Thus it was that, almost before he knew it, von Dodenburg had led them into high fen-bog, typical of the area – a series of snow-covered reed banks, under which the marsh squelched and quaked alarmingly. Von Dodenburg relaxed the pace, warning the men to close up and take care where they placed their feet.

He knew that these high marshes were exceedingly treacherous. They could swallow up a man in a flash, if he were unlucky enough to tread in the wrong place.

Gingerly, the sweat standing out on their foreheads like opaque pearls in spite of the freezing cold, the anxious troopers followed their C.O., edging their way from one reed-bank to another, listening to the marsh rumble and gurgle ominously beneath their feet.

Von Dodenburg took all the risks upon himself. Whenever he came to a particularly dangerous stretch, where he sensed the deadly mixture of muck and water was just below the surface of the snow, he stopped the column and went on by himself, trying to keep his balance, arms extended like a tight-rope artiste. It all looked very harmless, perhaps even a little silly, but von Dodenburg knew these high marshes. One slip from solid ground and he might well be up to his waist in the treacherous slime and a moment later he would be gone for ever. Time dragged as they crept across that lethal terrain. All talk ceased. Even Schulze was too fearful to speak. Instead all of them, as weary as they were, concentrated on the next metre of ground, heads cocked, tensed for the first sign or sound which would indicate that the surface of the snow was giving beneath them.

The storm abated gradually. A pale yellow, wintry sun began to appear. Its rays blinded them as they were reflected from the gleaming surface of the snowfield. It was painful to look up; the sun stabbed at their eyes like the blade of a sharp knife. Not that von Dodenburg dared look up much. His whole attention was concentrated on the treacherous ground beneath his feet, his body lathered with sweat, his clothes clinging to him unpleasantly. Desperately he prayed that they would be through the damned bog and reach the cover of the forest beyond before the *Ami* planes took to the sky again.

Now he could just make out the first of the snow-capped trees of the forest. His spirits rose. They were going to make it! By nightfall, with a bit of luck, they would reach Schloss Falkenstein. He started to take chances, forced on him by the urgency of reaching cover soon. The sun was getting stronger and it wouldn't be long before the *Ami* flyboys down on the plain scrambled their planes to search again for Wotan.

Suddenly the ground simply disappeared from under him. One moment he was treading gingerly over a patch of thin snow; the next he was sinking into the freezing icy mud beneath, his scream cut off by the shock of that freezingly cold mud. He tried to keep cool, knowing that he had only seconds to make the right decision. His men shouted in alarm as Schulze bellowed some sort of order, caught by surprise just as the rest had been. He forced himself to turn round and flop in the stinking greedy mud, arms outstretched like someone doing the breaststroke, nostrils assailed by the stench of the bog, now only millimetres from his face. For what seemed ages he simply lay there, hardly daring to breathe, knowing that the slightest wrong move might well mean the end; the mud would swallow him up in its greedy, stinking maws in an instant.

'Sir!' It was Schulze, staring down at him a little helplessly. 'What are we supposed to do?'

A hot retort sprang to his mind, but von Dodenburg controlled himself just in time. There must be no panic. Everything had to be thought out calmly, though he had never felt less like being calm and rational. 'Tell the men to stay exactly where they are. No one is to come any closer. Clear?'

'Clear, sir, but how are we going . . .'

'No buts. Just do as I say.' Around him the marsh began to squeak and groan as if it were a live thing, eager to swallow him. 'Take off your belts. Try to make some sort of rope. When I say "go" toss it to me, and for God's sake don't miss my hands!'

'We won't, sir. *We won't!*' Schulze called earnestly, his big face twisted with conflicting emotions as he stared down at his beloved C.O. 'Honest, we won't!'

'I know I can rely on you, you big rogue,' von Dodenburg said carefully, as the bog again groaned ominously. 'All right, get that rope prepared – *quick!*' he squeezed out the command in near panic.

Schulze disappeared, already ripping at his belt. Minutes – to von Dodenburg it seemed an eternity – passed as the men fumbled with icy fingers to link their belts together, before Schulze reappeared.

'Don't be a nervous old hen,' von Dodenburg attempted to reassure him. 'I'll be all right. Are you ready?'

'Yes sir. Ready.'

'Good, then don't come any closer. Throw me the rope.'

Schulze swallowed hard. Von Dodenburg could see his Adam's apple slide up and down his throat as if it were an express lift. 'I'm throwing now, sir.' Schulze took a deep breath and launched the awkward rope towards the trapped officer.

It dropped – *centimetres short of von Dodenburg's right hand*! Schulze groaned out loud and punched his throwing arm angrily. Von Dodenburg hesitated. Dare he move? Would the damned slime swallow him up the moment he made an attempt to reach out for the belt, so tantalizingly close, yet as far away as the moon.

Above him Schulze agonized, the sweat standing out in beads on his contorted face.

Slowly, very slowly, von Dodenburg started to raise his right hand out of the mud. Greedily, it gurgled and clung to his arm so that he had to exert more pressure to free himself. With a reluctant sucking, slithering noise, the swamp let go. Von Dodenburg gasped. His heart was racing madly. The sweat poured down his mud-encrusted face.

'All right, sir?' Schulze whispered apprehensively. By an effort of sheer naked willpower, he forced himself to answer, 'Yes, yes, I'm all right, Schulze.' He licked his caked lips and would have given a fortune at that moment for a stiff slug of schnapps. Fingers outspread, he began to edge his hand forward to the end of the belt-rope, his breath coming in short gasps, his eyes fixed hypnotically on the bubbling mud.

'You're doing it, sir,' Schulze whispered hoarsely. 'Only a matter of millimetres . . . .' He broke off with a gasp. The mud had given suddenly. In a flash, more of von Dodenburg's lower body disappeared into the grey slime. Matz stifled a cry of alarm. Next to him the little *Luftwaffe* pilot hissed, 'He's had it. The marsh's got him!'

'*Schnauze*!' Matz growled. 'Hold yer friggin' water, or I'll friggin' well carve yer mesen!' He looked down at the C.O. trapped in the mud, lying perfectly immobile now, head bent as if in defeat, tears filling his bloodshot eyes.

For what seemed an age, no one spoke, no one moved. They seemed frozen there like characters in some third-rate melodrama just before the curtain goes down at the end of the act. Then Schulze broke the tense silence with a gruff, 'Sir, sir.'

Slowly von Dodenburg raised his mud-encrusted face, eyes glowing like coals in that mask of mud. 'Yes?' he said quietly, as if he were infinitely weary. 'Yes?'

'You've nearly done it, sir. Just one more try; one more try and you're home and dry, sir.' There was a note of pleading in the NCO's voice and the tears were streaming down his face. '*You've got to!*'

'I can't, Schulze. I can't!' It seemed to take the trapped

officer an eternity to get the words out. 'I'm . . . absolutely
. . . knackered.'

Schulze swallowed hard. 'But you've got to try, sir. *You've
got to!*' Even as he spoke the mud bubbled and gurgled in
triumph, sensing now that it had won the battle; that soon it
would devour the body of this mortal who had had the
temerity to venture into its kingdom.

Von Dodenburg's eyes closed, as if in resignation. He made
no answer to Schulze's impassioned appeal. Schulze stared
at him, as if he could not believe the evidence of his own eyes.
The C.O. had never given in. Somehow, even when they had
been in the worst of situations, he had rallied, forced himself
to carry on, to win through. 'But, sir, we *need* you! The lads
need you! Without you Wotan is finished. We'll never get out
of these frigging mountains!'

Slowly von Dodenburg opened his eyes and stared blindly
up at Schulze, as if he was no part of whatever was happening
at this moment, as if he simply could not take it in.

Schulze tried again. 'Sir.' The hysteria had vanished from
his voice now. He had a firm grip on himself once more.
'Wotan, sir. Remember? Wotan needs you.' He repeated the
name, emphasizing it as if it were of great significance. '*Wotan!*'

The dazed look vanished from the trapped man's eyes.
'Wotan,' he echoed, his mud-encrusted lips working, as if
activated by rusty springs. For a moment von Dodenburg lay
there, while Schulze stared at him desperately, willing him to
move. What was the C.O. thinking? What was going through
his mind at this moment? Had the name conjured up
memories of the great days when those blond young giants
had marched so proudly through the streets of the Reich,
bellowing out that bold marching song of SS Wotan? Was he
thinking of those desperate battles on the frozen steppes in
Russia? The burning heat of the African desert? Were all the
memories of five long years of war, all those blond young men
who had come to Wotan to learn to fight – and die – fusing
together in his mind to make him act?

Schulze did not know. Nor did he care. *Slowly, painfully*

slowly, the C.O. was beginning to move once more. His appeal had paid off. The C.O. was trying to free himself!

Behind Schulze the horrified troopers watched the progress in tense silence. Even the trembling of their frozen limbs had ceased. Nothing existed in the world but the feeble, terribly slow, movements of the man trapped in that treacherous slime. Von Dodenburg's mind worked with electric speed. He could feel his nerve endings jingle. His every sense was once more acute, tensed for the first sign that the treacherous mud was again attempting to devour him. Schulze and the men had formed a loop in the end of the belt rope. He would have to raise himself slightly to slip the loop around his chest – once he had got hold of it. But could he chance it? He was like some pathetic dying beetle floating on the surface of the water, held there against all the laws of gravity. One awkward move and the mud would have him. The swamp – cold, cruel and inhumane as it was – would not give him a second chance.

'Damn you!' He cursed the mud under his nose, as if it were a living thing. 'You're not going to have me!' Next moment the tips of his outstretched fingers touched the cold metal of a belt buckle. He had reached the crude leather rope!

Von Dodenburg swallowed hard. Gently he shook his head to dislodge the pearls of sweat that had dropped to his eyebrows and were threatening to blind him. It was now or never. He began to raise his chest, desperately clinging on to the rope. The swamp gurgled and his nostrils were assailed by the sulphurous odour of marsh gas. Again he heard the silver blare of the brass, the proud shrill note of the bugles, the harsh stamp of eight hundred pairs of steel-shod boots on the cobbles: Wotan in the great days, always victorious, the elite of the elite, Germany's finest, Hitler's own Black Guards. After all that and what had come later, was he going to allow himself to die here, in this filthy arsehole of a place, which did not even have a name?

His fears vanished and he began to slide the rope under his chest. Above him Schulze willed him to succeed, his fists balled into great threatening clubs.

'There . . .' von Dodenburg began, but the surface of the
swamp opened up that very instant and his sudden scream of
alarm was cut off by the choking mud as his head disappeared
under the black and stinking morass.

'*He's going!*' Matz screamed.

'*Fuck that for a tale!*' Schulze bellowed. He grabbed the belt
rope, praying fervently that it wouldn't break, and heaved.
Behind him the ashen-faced troopers sprang into action and
caught hold of the rope.

Von Dodenburg's head was barely visible now. The mud
gurgled and bubbled. It nearly had him.

'Put yer frigging backs into it!' Matz cursed. '*Pull!*'

With all their might, the veins standing out on their faces
like purple wires, their breath coming in short harsh gasps,
the troopers heaved. But the marsh fought back. Great
bubbles of marsh gas kept rising, and exploded to fill the air
with their noxious stench. The whole surface of the swamp
trembled and swayed like the rumblings of some great gas-
distended stomach. Tenaciously it held on to its victim,
determined not to be cheated of its prey.

Schulze, his chest heaving with the effort, and the muscles
rippling down his brawny arms like steel cables, could see the
slime clinging to von Dodenburg's body, hanging on and
refusing to surrender the C.O. to his desperate men.

'Once again!' he yelled. 'Give it all you've got, lads. *Heave!*'
They heaved. For what seemed an age, nothing happened.
The men fought the mud with the last of their fast-ebbing
strength.

Suddenly there was a loud sucking noise. With a huge pop,
like a reluctant cork finally being pulled, von Dodenburg shot
out of the mud to land on solid ground gasping and choking
for breath like a stranded fish, hardly daring to believe that he
had escaped that terrible fate.

Five minutes later they were running desperately for the
cover of the forest as the first of those deadly silver birds came
winging in from the west seeking them anew.

CHAPTER 7

'Well, they can't have simply vanished into thin air, Wolf,' Colonel Petersen exclaimed in exasperation and ran his hand through his greying crew-cut hair, as the staff crowded around the maps spread out on the farmhouse kitchen table.

The remote farm's outhouses were packed with Petersen's weary, frozen soldiers, trying to get warm by burrowing into the stiff straw, others cooking little cans of hash and spam over fires made from the cardboard containers in which the C rations came. Others were too weary to do anything but lie on the dirt floor, still clad in full combat gear, and fall into an exhausted sleep. The last two days of pursuit had taken it out of Petersen's 'Fighting Coons'. As Master-Sergeant Lee had reported to Petersen with a wry grin, 'Colonel, suh, this snow and these mountains sure have done knocked the piss-and-vinegar out of the men!' Petersen had been forced to agree. Most of the poor bastards – virtually eighty per cent of his men were from the Deep South – had never even *seen* snow before until this week!

He cast an angry glance out of the dirty window at the flakes which had begun to fall again and snapped, 'I know they're the SS and all that kinda crap, Wolf, but even those SS jerks can't stand it much longer in this kind of hellish weather!'

Wolf nodded in agreement. 'Yes sir, that's true. They've been on the run for over three days now. The food they stole in Ste Marie must be exhausted by now.' He shrugged, his cunning face puzzled. 'But, this morning, when Air did manage to fly, the pilots reported nothing. *Zilch*!'

Petersen sucked his teeth, while his officers waited. On the wall a cheap cuckoo clock from the neighbouring *Schwarzwald* ticked away the seconds of their lives with metallic inexorability. 'So where they're at? It's colder than a witch's tit out there!

They must have gone to ground somewhere, *but where*?' he asked a little hopelessly. 'That's the goddam sixty-four dollar question!'

On the wall, the garishly painted cuckoo popped out of his box and sounded the hour. Petersen looked at the wooden bird as if he might draw his 45 at any moment and blow it into the courtyard outside. Wolf grinned guardedly. Petersen was straining at the leash. He wanted to do something, *anything*! But he simply didn't know where to start.

'Sir, there is no other way for it. The flyboys say they are simply not going to fly in a white-out like this. It's too risky.'

'Sure,' Petersen commented sourly, as the cuckoo disappeared – as if it somehow sensed what was going on in the irate officer's mind. 'Yeah, nice and warm, shooting the breeze back in coca-cola land and playing poker, that's your frigging pilots for you!'

'If they won't fly, we've got to continue the search ourselves,' said Wolf.

Petersen flashed him a bitter look. 'My men wouldn't object, believe you me, Wolf. They'd go if I ordered them to.'

Master-Sergeant Lee shook his head in mock disbelief. The Old Man really did believe the sun shone out of the black assholes of his men!

'But in this weather, Wolf.' He shrugged. 'They simply aren't used to snow. It's something that goes with white folks' Christmas parties, that's all. Most of them have never seen the damned stuff until these last few days.'

'I understand that, sir,' Wolf agreed. 'But there is a vehicle called the Weasel which should help to solve that particular problem, sir.'

'The Weasel?'

'Yes sir. It's something new in the Army, although it was developed back in 'forty when they started to build the Alaskan Highway. A rubber-tracked vehicle that can carry six or seven men and can move easily over snow, swamp, you name it, the lot.'

'And we've got it?' Petersen asked.

'You're darned right, sir. At first light I called the Chief-of-Intelligence at Seventh Army HQ and told him our problem. He promised *personally* that he would have a convoy of Weasels – enough to move your whole battalion – on their way to us within the hour.' Wolf looked at his wrist-watch. 'That was three hours or more ago. With luck they should be reaching us soon, complete with drivers.'

Petersen smiled at him and then asked, strangely enough, '*Black* drivers, for these Weasels of yours, I mean?'

'I wouldn't know about that, sir. As the dog-faces say, sir, that would be asking for eggs in your beer as well.'

'Yeah, I guess you're right there, Wolf. Okay, then we'll let the men rest for another two hours. Got that, Sergeant Lee?'

'Yes sir.'

'Then,' Petersen's face grew grim and determined, 'we're gonna find those SS bastards, even if we've got to go to the end of the world to do so.'

'God Almighty!' Schulze exclaimed in awe, 'what's a place like that doing here, at the end of the frigging world?'

Together with the rest of the weary Wotan troopers, he stumbled to a halt and stared at the strange sight which had appeared so suddenly in the middle of this snowy wilderness. On the other side of the valley, perched on a wooded hill, there it was: Schloss Falkenstein, a turreted mediaeval castle brooding above the snow-bound valley in gaunt isolation.

Von Dodenburg licked his lips and stared at the castle, his mind wondering what secrets it held in store for SS Assault Regiment Wotan. He realized that Himmler was not concerned solely with rescuing what was left of Wotan; he had other plans for it. For a few moments he continued to stare at the silent castle on the other side of the valley, his professional ye telling him that it was beautifully sited for defence. There was a single steep track leading up to it, with slopes to left and right, absolutely bare of cover. Even five

hundred years after the place had been built, it would be a
tough nut to crack. Aircraft would be of little use to the
attackers. The walls were obviously immensely thick; and
castles of that kind always had a whole rabbit warren of deep,
well-protected cellars beneath them. No, he concluded, he
wouldn't like the task of attacking Schloss Falkenstein, even
in 1944.

'All right, Schulze, let's get on with it. Get the men moving
again.'

'Yes, sir,' Schulze said, full of life again, and von
Dodenburg knew why. The big rogue was already visualizing
the beer he would drink there and the women he would
'pleasure', as he always put it in his usual, modest manner.

The same sort of thoughts must have animated the weary
troopers too, for they quickened their pace, seeming not to
notice the knee-deep snow of the long slope that led down into
the valley they must cross before they reached Schloss
Falkenstein.

Up front, just behind von Dodenburg, Schulze was in high
good humour, boring Matz, as usual, with his impossible
anecdotes, which were all centred on women or drink or both.
'I once knew a feller,' he boomed happily, 'who kept a whore
with a wooden leg. But all the same he didn't trust her one bit,
you know, Matzi. Kept her leg in a cupboard at night just to
make sure she didn't hop it while he was asleep. Don't yer get
it – a one-legged women *hopping* it? Ha, ha!'

'Yer,' Matz replied, bored. 'Very funny indeed. I'm pissing
mesen with laughter, can't yer hear?' But his old running-
mate was not going to let his good humour be dampened by
Matz's sour reply.

'Still, she went and hoofed it on him. Somebody had gone
and given her another wooden leg. Now what do you say to
that, Matzi?' He went on, without waiting for his comrade's
reaction. 'And do you know what she wrote on the note to
him that she left behind?'

'No, but you'll tell me,' Matz said sourly.

'The new one's got a better knee action, Hans. You can

keep the old one!' Schulze gave a great hoarse laugh. 'Now she was a cheeky piece of gash, wasn't she?'

Still Matz was unimpressed. 'The only thing you can do to keep a dame from getting up to tricks would be to take *that* off'n her,' he said grimly. 'And so far nobody's come up with an idea for how to do it.'

Von Dodenburg grinned. The two rogues were in fine form once again, the trials and tribulations of the last few days obviously forgotten.

'I once knew a dentist who had false teeth,' Schulze started off again, overlooking Matz's bored look.

'That's funny for a start. A tooth merchant with false biters. Ha, *fuckin*' ha!'

'No, no, that's not it,' Schulze said. 'No, you see it was the way he used to get his jollies when he'd had a bit o' sauce. Well, when he was half-pissed, he'd take out his top and bottom sets and try to bit off the nipples of the whore he was with with them! That was it. That's all he wanted. Nothing else.'

Even Matz was impressed. 'You mean he had this piece of steaming gash and all he wanted was to play around with his biters on her tits?'

'Of course the whore had to have plenty of wood in front of the door so that he could get his choppers on 'em. But that was all he ever wanted.'

Matz shook his head. 'Ever since Christ was a carpenter, that's the weirdest I've ever heard of.'

Again von Dodenburg shook his head and tried to forget the excited talk behind him, as the long column worked its way down the slope, up to their knees in the snow. Now they could see the castle in detail and it was clear that it was occupied. Smoke drifted leisurely from the pointed slate towers into the dawn sky, and there was a muted hammering sound like someone striking metal. Faintly von Dodenburg could smell what he took to be burnt paint, the kind of odour he remembered from the tank workshops back in the Reich. He rubbed his chin and wondered what was going on up there. Behind him, Schulze suddenly forgot the whore with the wooden leg and the dentist with strange sexual tastes and said, 'Who do you think they are up there, sir?'

Von Dodenburg shrugged, not taking his gaze off the castle. He had just caught the bright glint of glass in the tower to the right and knew they were being observed. 'All I know is that Herr Himmler has ordered me to report to a Colonel von Falkenstein. My guess is that he is some sort of local aristocracy, probably from the family which owns the schloss.'

'Aristocracy!' Schulze echoed, impressed. 'Did you hear that, plush-arse?'

'I heard,' Matz answered. 'So what am I supposed to do? Have me frigging monthlies?'

'Knock off that frigging coarse talk, arse-with-ears, or you'll get a frigging knuckle sandwich in zero, comma, nothing, seconds!' Schulze threatened, clenching his fist. 'You're gonna meet posh folk soon. So don't forget to stick out yer little pinkie when you're drinking china tea out of them porcelain cups.'

'Oh, go and piss in the wind!' Matz snorted. 'What do you think them posh folk do? Shit through the ribs, perhaps?'

The unassailable logic of that stopped even Schulze, so they ploughed out through the glittering snowfield in silence, every eye fixed on the castle now, as the unknown watcher followed their progress to Schloss Falkenstein.

'Hey you, boy!' the driver of the first little squat tracked vehicle called from his cab as the leading Weasel came to a halt in the farmyard. He pointed his finger at Master-Sergeant Lee and called again. 'Hey you, black boy, I'm talking to ya, or are ya deef?' The accent was one hundred per cent Georgia.

Lee looked at the burly white corporal stonily. 'Are you talking to me, Corporal?' he asked, keeping his voice under control by an effort of will. 'If you are, then hang a "sergeant" on to it, *quick*!'

'You're only a nigger sergeant,' the corporal sneered, as more and more of the little vehicles came to a halt and their white drivers got out to stare at Lee as if he were some sort of circus animal. 'Nigger sergeants don't count no more than a buck private, if he's white, that is.' He grinned at the others and winked knowingly.

Lee fought back his rage. He would have dearly loved to have dropped his pistol belt and waded into the big ugly redneck. But he couldn't do that to Colonel Petersen. He had to stay calm and do this thing in US Army style, according to the book. 'Report to the C.O. at once,' he ordered. 'He's waiting for you. He's over there in that farmhouse.'

The Corporal didn't move. Instead he said, affecting mock surprise. 'Are you giving *me*,' he jerked a big thumb at his chest, 'orders, *nigger*?' he demanded.

'No, he is not,' Captain Wolf's cool New England voice cut in. '*I am!*'

The NCO spun round, face flushed purple, little red eyes glinting dangerously, fists clenched. He opened his mouth to speak and then, at the sight of the tarnished silver captain's bars, he closed it again.

'Well?' Wolf demanded.

For one long moment, while Lee tensed, ready to spring into action, the Corporal glared at the little Jewish Captain as if he might well refuse. Then he let his shoulders slump.

'Okay, you guys, get ready to load up.'

'But Mel,' one of them cried in protest. 'We ain't gonna have to play choffer for a bunch of negras, have we?'

'Yeah,' someone else agreed. 'Back home my mammy wouldn't even allow me to spit on no negra – never mind drive the mothers!'

'Do as you're told,' the Corporal growled and walked away, muttering to himself about 'kikes' and 'goddam black niggers'.

Wolf watched him go. He told himself there was going to be trouble with the white drivers, if Colonel Petersen wasn't too careful.

Next to him Lee relaxed. With a lazy grin, he said, 'Thanks Captain, but you know, sir, that white trash just missed having his head blown off,' he touched his low-slung forty-five significantly, 'by about thirty seconds.'

Wolf grinned too; then he was business-like again. 'Tell the C.O. the Weasels are here.'

'Sir!'

'And Sergeant Lee.'

'Sir.'

Wolf hesitated a moment before saying quietly, 'Warn your fellahs. Those drivers are bad news.'

Lee nodded. 'Yeah, I know what you mean. It's goddam bad enough fighting those Krauts, but when you've got to fight your own people as well . . .' He shrugged and turned. Without another word, he strode away to carry out Wolf's orders, leaving the latter staring at his broad back and wondering what was going on in Lee's black head at that moment.

CHAPTER 8

'What do you think, sir?' Schulze asked, as the column came to a halt beneath the castle.

Von Dodenburg frowned. Whoever inhabited Schloss Falkenstein was apparently making no attempt to greet the weary strangers. 'I don't quite know, Schulze,' he answered slowly, running his gaze over the terrain to left and right of the path which led to the house and which had recently been cleared of snow. He indicated the skull-and-crossbone signs protruding above the snowfield to their right. 'Look at that.'

'Mined! The fields are mined.'

'Yes, and up there to the right at three o'clock. That's obviously a bunker. Probably a machine gun in it covering this path.'

Schulze nodded in agreement. 'Yes, but where are the frigging natives, and where's this local aristocrat, sir?'

'Well, there's only one way to find out, isn't there, Schulze?'

'But I mean, sir,' Schulze answered uneasily, 'you can't just go up to the front door like and ask if anybody's at home, can you?'

'I don't know of any other way,' von Dodenburg replied with forced cheerfulness. For he had an uneasy sensation that they were being watched by unseen eyes all the time and felt a cold finger of fear trace its way down the small of his back. He shivered.

'All right,' he snapped, telling himself that he was behaving like a nervous schoolgirl, 'you come with me, Schulze. Corporal Matz, you take over. Form a defensive perimeter, *just in case*!'

'Sir!' Matz answered smartly and began rapping out his orders.

Schulze unslung his Schmeisser and clicked off the 'safety' significantly. 'I'm ready when you are, sir,' he said.

Von Dodenburg nodded and flipped open the leather cover of his pistol holster. Schulze was right. They might well be walking straight into a trap. 'All right, let's dance.'

Schulze gave him a wary smile. 'I've got my party frock on already, sir.'

They moved off. Behind them Matz called softly, 'And Schulze, don't forget to tip the butler when he opens the door for yer.'

'Butler, my ass!' Schulze sneered, but his heart wasn't in it. There was something too eerie about the Gothic castle which rose above them for his usual banter.

In grim silence the two of them started to walk up the path cleared of snow. To right and left the rusty wire bore the signs warning of mines, but otherwise there was still no sign that the house was occupied, save for that muted hammering sound which von Dodenburg had heard earlier. Systematically he searched the crumbling grey stone front of the castle for any token of life; but there was none. All the ground floor windows were barred and shuttered. On the second floor, the tall leaded windows revealed nothing.

Suddenly von Dodenburg felt his nerves begin to flutter. What in the devil's name was going on in Schloss Falkenstein?

Schulze, obviously similarly affected by this strange silent place, licked his lips and whispered, 'I wish the frig somebody'd turn up, even if it's only to say fuck off!' Silently von Dodenburg agreed.

The door was huge and made of oak, the usual legend in Alsatian-German carved above it, worn by the years so that it was no longer possible to read it. But the coat-of-arms was clear enough – a shield with a single SS rune like a jagged bolt of lightning running through it, above the legend '*Schlag Zuruck*'.

Von Dodenburg looked up at it. ' "Strike Back", eh? Some motto,' he mused. 'Obviously a very warlike gentleman, our Colonel von Falkenstein. Schulze whipped the dewdrop hanging from his red nose expertly away and tossed it in the snow.

'There's somebody watching us sir,' he hissed. 'Top

window right – and he's armed. Unless that's an erection he's carrying in his hands.'

'Doubt it,' von Dodenburg said. 'All right, here we go!' Forcing himself not to look up at the window, he pulled the rusting bell wire. There came the muffled tolling of a bell, which echoed and re-echoed in the remote recesses of the castle. For what seemed a long time nothing happened. Next to von Dodenburg, Schulze shivered and jerked his Schmeisser up and down, as if he would dearly love to let off a blast and break the intolerable tension. Then they became aware of the footsteps coming towards the great door.

'Someone's coming!' Schulze hissed unnecessarily.

Von Dodenburg swallowed hard. The door was beginning to swing open. The smell, a mixture of furniture polish and age-old mysteries, assailed von Dodenburg's nostrils. An old man stood there, white-gloved and wearing a bow-tie above his striped waistcoat, bowing slightly as he saw the ragged visitors.

'Welcome to Schloss Falkenstein, gentlemen,' he croaked, smiling slightly to reveal yellowed, ill-fitting false teeth. 'Colonel von Falkenstein is expecting you.'

Schulze's mouth dropped open. 'Christ on a crutch,' he gasped. 'A real butler, just like Matzi said. *Wow*!'

The servant did not seem to notice the NCO's surprise. Instead he opened the great door wider and bowed again, indicating with his gloved hand that they should enter. 'This way, please, *meine Herren*,' and, without waiting for them to reply, he began to waddle forward down the dark corridor, his shoes creaking on the polished floor boards.

Schulze looked at von Dodenburg and then at the butler already disappearing into the gloom of the corridor. 'What do you think, sir?' he whispered. 'Shall we follow?'

Von Dodenburg motioned with his hand towards the top of a staircase to their right. 'I don't think we've any alternative, Schulze,' he said softly.

Schulze gasped. Above them were half-a-dozen civilians, dressed in rough work clothes, their round peasant faces set and grim, all of them holding shotguns which were aimed directly at the two men. And there was no doubt about it: they would blast the two of them into eternity at the first wrong move.

'Holy strawsack!' Schulze whispered. 'The reception committee – and from the look on their ugly mugs, I don't think they overly like us.'

They followed the butler as he led them down corridor after corridor, lined with faded portraits of earlier von Falkensteins and yellowing photographs of 19th-century worthies, complete with high stiff collars and countenances full of even higher moral superiority. 'Like a frigging museum!' was Schulze's scornful comment. 'God, what a dump!'

They came at last to a great panelled hall, the thin yellow rays of the winter sun streaming through the tall leaded windows, a massive log fire crackling brightly in the open hearth, the whole place suddenly warm and inviting, a complete contrast from the gloomy corridors through which they had passed to reach it.

'Please wait one moment, *meine Herren*,' the old butler commanded, 'until I inform the Colonel.'

Schulze headed straight for the fire and, jerking up the rear of his ragged tunic, pointed his rump at the flames, sighing in delight. 'Lovely. Lovely grub. Almost as good as dipping it in a lovely hot juicy honeypot!' He closed his eyes, a look of absolute delight on his broad face.

Von Dodenburg knew what Schulze meant. For the first time in nearly two months of constant combat and retreat, they at last had found themselves under a roof in a civilized place, warm and comfortable, with the prospect of more good things, in the shape of hot food and drink, to come. It was almost too much to bear. He, too, stretched out his hands towards the crackling flames, feeling the heat surge through his frozen limbs. God, wasn't it damn good!

'*Meine Herren*!' It was the ancient butler again. He was standing by the entrance to the big room with what appeared to be the suspicion of a grin on his wizened old face. 'Will you

please come this way?' he announced, and again von
Dodenburg felt he was laughing at them. 'The Colonel will
receive you now.'

Schulze hated to give up the fire, but already the C.O. was
striding towards the door, so he let his tunic fall back over his
delightfully warm buttocks and followed reluctantly. They
trailed after the old man down another long, gloomy corridor
until finally he paused in front of a door and knocked politely.
There was a slight pause, then a deep voice, which sounded as
if it was used to giving orders and having them obeyed,
commanded, 'Come!'

The butler opened the door and announced, '*Obersturmbannführer* von Dodenburg and companion.' He looked at Schulze
a little uncertainly. Schulze jerked up his dirty middle finger
and silently mouthed the words, 'Sit on this, shiteheel!'

They entered the room and found themselves in a big
study. The walls were adorned with swords and old-fashioned
horse pistols; tattered regimental banners hung from the high
ceiling. In front of a big desk which dominated the room, an
evil-looking black Doberman growled warningly, baring its
fangs. Von Dodenburg clicked to attention, ignoring the dog,
'*Obersturmbannführer von Dodenburg meldet sich zur Stelle!*' he
barked, using the accepted military formula.

The unseen Colonel von Falkenstein (for the back of the big
desk chair was turned to face the door of the study) said
pleasantly, though the voice was one hundred per cent
Prussian, 'Why so formal, Colonel? Please stand at ease.'

The two SS men relaxed as Colonel von Falkenstein's chair
slowly swivelled round to face them.

Von Dodenburg gasped, while Schulze, gaping like some
village idiot, muttered, 'Well, I'll go an' shit a brick!'

Colonel von Falkenstein grinned and leaned back in the
big chair. In doing so the red-and-blue embroidered dressing
gown slipped open to reveal a long stretch of exquisite thigh,
clad in sheer black stocking.

*Colonel von Falkenstein, whom they had come so far to meet, was a
woman.*

BOOK THREE

The Castle of the Damned

'What of the faith and fire within us – men who march away?'

Thomas Hardy.

CHAPTER 1

It was dawn and the snow had stopped falling. To the Battalion's front the pure white carpet of snow stretched to the horizon where the sun was already poised above the crest of the mountains. There was little sound, save that of weary men slowly waking up to another long, cold day. Here and there one of Petersen's black soldiers was heating up a can of hash over a flickering fire of cardboard and twigs. But most of them were content with a canteen of black coffee; C rations at this time of the morning had little appeal to them.

Wolf found the view serene and beautiful, as if the war were a million miles away and not just over the other side of those mountains, down on the Rhine. But it was also damnably cold. He shivered and looked forward to the warmth of the Weasels, once their drivers got them started up. He glanced over to where the white drivers huddled around a fire, drinking their coffee in gloomy silence, well away from Petersen's men. Even now, after two days of searching for the elusive SS men, they had not come to terms with the fact that the men they were carrying were American soldiers, too, fighting the same enemy. They were constantly grumbling and complaining. Their NCO and natural leader, Corporal Melgrove ('Big Red' his drivers called him, on account of his fiery hair and even more fiery temper) was the worst of the lot. He bitched all the time about the indignity of having to drive 'a bunch of coons' all over the 'goddam frog countryside'. He had even had the nerve to make a formal protest to Colonel Petersen, stating bluntly that he would report 'this insult to the white race' – those were the words he had used – to his commanding officer once he returned to the depot.

Petersen had fallen on him like a ton of bricks. 'One more word out of you, Corporal!' he had snapped, his eyes flashing fire, 'and you can consider yourself stripped of your stripes.

You'll be a buck private before you know what's hit you!'

Big Red had opened his mouth to make some angry retort, but had thought better of it. He had walked away, fists clenched, full of repressed anger at what he obviously considered to be the betrayal of the white race by the 'nigger-loving Colonel'.

As the first of Petersen's men began to buckle on their combat gear, Wolf, his hands clasping the hot metal of his canteen cup as if his very life depended upon it, saw that Big Red's drivers were not making a move. Yet they all knew that in these sub-zero conditions it took a good five or ten minutes to start up their little tracked vehicles. He frowned. What was the bigoted redneck up to? Five minutes later he found out. Petersen, irritated by the fact that the Weasels were not already warming up, marched over the crisp snow and barked, 'Well, Corporal, do you need a goddam written invitation? Why aren't you moving?'

Big Red continued to glower into his canteen, while the rest of the unshaven drivers squatted round the fire, pretending not to notice Petersen's presence.

Petersen flushed angrily. 'Are you damned deaf, Corporal?' he demanded. 'And when I speak to you, get to your feet!'

Slowly, reluctantly, Big Red rose to his feet, a sneer of contempt on his ugly piglike face. Still he did not speak.

'Well?' an exasperated Petersen exclaimed. 'What's it going to be?' The southerner gave the New England Colonel a look of undisguised hate. 'Well, where I come from, Colonel, *sir*,' he emphasized the 'sir' scornfully, 'we don't have no truck with nigger trash. And that goes for the guys, too.' There was a murmur of agreement from the other drivers.

'I am not one bit interested in your native prejudices,' Petersen snapped, keeping his temper under control with difficulty. 'All I am asking – no, *ordering* – you to do is to keep those damned vehicles started, toot-sweet!'

Big Red sucked his rotten teeth and said, 'We're not gonna do it. We're not gonna drive for those lowdown niggers.'

He blurted the words out defiantly. 'And you can court-martial me if you like, 'cos I'm still not gonna fart around waiting hand an' foot on niggers. Besides,' he added slyly, 'you gonna have to court-martial the whole shoot of us, colonel, *sir.*'

He grinned at the others, who grinned back, sure of their position. It wouldn't look good in any officer's records to have been a party to the court-martialling of over thirty white soldiers in a colour-prejudiced US Army.

Wolf's eyes narrowed to slits. The cunning bastards! They'd obviously been discussing this among themselves for some time. Military justice was clearly on Colonel Petersen's side, but they knew the Regular Army. Sentiment and emotion were clearly against Petersen. Wolf looked at the tall, skinny Colonel. How was he going to get out of this one? Even if he arrested the drivers, he still couldn't make them drive? And his 'coons', unmechanical as most of them were, would be unable to drive the tricky little tracked vehicles with their complicated gear system.

For what seemed a long time Colonel Petersen did not speak or move. He continued to stare at Big Red, as if he were seeing him for the first time, as the grin of contempt on the latter's ugly face grew ever broader. The southerner reckoned he had Colonel Petersen by the short and curlies, but he was mistaken. He had not gauged the full determination of the New Englander. Probably he thought of him contemptuously as yet another of those soft nigger-loving trouble-makers from north of the Mason-Dixon Line who was all 'mouth' and little else.

Finally Petersen spoke. 'You realize, don't you, Corporal,' he said quietly, 'that you are on active service?'

'Yeah, sure, but what has that got to do . . .'

'In essence you are refusing an order,' Colonel Petersen cut him short, 'while confronting the enemy. I believe the manual calls it "*in the face* of the enemy".'

Big Red stared at the Colonel, bewildered by this unexpected turn of events. Behind him his drivers looked at

one another as Big Red licked his lips, suddenly deflated. This
was not the same tough-talking, boastful Corporal Melgrove
who had told them that his plan was foolproof; nothing could
go wrong. The 'nigger-lover' was going to have to do as they
wanted, if he didn't want to get 'shafted' by the top brass.

'I believe that there is not a court-martial anywhere in the
world, where the US Army is currently in combat, which
would not accept that I have ample justification for what I am
now about to do,' Petersen continued, flipping open his
holster and taking out his forty-five Colt.

'Do what?' Big Red muttered, suddenly afraid of the look
on Petersen's face.

'What?' Petersen asked. 'Why, shoot you, that's what.'

Big Red gasped. '*Shoot me?*' he stuttered, his big paws
fluttering upwards as if he were physically trying to ward off
the steel slugs.

'Yes.' Petersen clicked off the 'safety'. 'All right, Corporal,
this is it. I am going to give you a direct order.'

A few yards away Master-Sergeant Lee, his gaze flashing
between Petersen and Big Red and the sullen drivers,
snapped, 'Detail, detail, *port arms!*'

Behind him a group of young black soldiers sprang to
attention and snapped their Garands across their chests
stiffly, as if they were the honour squad back at Fort Benning.
To make it quite clear to the other drivers what was going to
happen to them if they attempted to interfere, Lee drew his own
forty-five and made a great show of clicking off the 'safety'.
Satisfied that they had got the message, he waited.

Petersen hesitated for an instant only; then he barked, his
voice crisp and commanding, 'Corporal, I am giving you a
direct order to start up your vehicles, *now!*'

Big Red licked his thick red lips, but still he did not move.
His mind was racing frantically, wondering how he could
back down in front of the niggers and what effect this would
have on his own men. What would they think of him if he
gave in to this nigger-loving, northern carpet-bagger?
Colonel Petersen did not give him any more time to consider.

The knuckles of his right hand whitened. He took first pressure. In another moment he would fire and at that range he couldn't miss. He would blast Big Red's chest wide open.

Suddenly all the fight went out of the corporal. '*Okay, okay*!' he shouted. 'I'm going. I'm going.' He turned and called sulkily, 'All right you guys, don't stand around waiting for the shit to hit the fan. Mount up, willya, for frig's sake. Mount up!' Without even looking at them, he flung open the door of the leading Weasel and thrust his bulk behind the driving wheel. Next moment he had started the engine, filling the dawn air with the stink of gasoline.

For a moment the other drivers simply stood there as if they could not quite comprehend what had happened; then they too began to drift sullenly towards their vehicles, their shoulders bent, as if in defeat.

For a few moments Wolf watched them go, as, behind him, Lee issued his orders in a subdued voice, as if he thought that it was not right, in view of what had just happened, to indulge in any kind of triumph. Then he walked over to Petersen, who had remained standing there, pistol still in hand. Wolf licked his lips. 'I think, sir,' he said carefully, and seeming to have difficulty in formulating his words, 'that you have made a bad enemy there.'

Petersen nodded, his eyes fixed on some distant object. 'I am sure you are right, Captain. What a goddam awful world it is where you have to threaten your fellow countrymen!' He shook his head and walked away without saying another word.

Wolf looked at Master-Sergeant Lee who was watching the Colonel, a look of almost dog-like affection in his gaze, and he realized that from now on someone was going to be watching Colonel Petersen's back, namely Master-Sergeant Lee. He nodded his head as if in approval and began to walk through the snow towards the waiting Weasels.

Five minutes later they had gone and the snowflakes were beginning to drift down once more, obliterating all signs that they had passed this way.

*

As that long day progressed and the column of Weasels zig-zagged across the frozen wastes of that desolate landscape in search of the elusive SS, Wolf realized that the die had been cast. It was nothing tangible, nothing he could put his finger on, but it was there all right.

Big Red and the other drivers remained obstinately silent; they no longer even cursed their lot and the 'niggers' they were forced to transport. But their mood was clear enough; it was one of sullen resentment, a furtive kind of hate that showed itself by an angry clash of gears or a sudden swerve of the vehicle to left or right, sending its occupants grabbing for support, a bitter look caught in the driving mirror for an instant.

Captain Wolf knew that Big Red and his comrades would never again chance a direct confrontation with Colonel Petersen, but that at the first opportunity they would bug out, leaving him and his men stranded up here in this godawful end of the world. Or perhaps even worse.

Wolf was overcome by a sense of impending disaster for Colonel Petersen and his 'Fighting Coons'. Try as he might, he could not shake it off. Something terrible was going to happen, he knew.

CHAPTER 2

She was clad in a black clinging suit which emphasized her startling figure. A fur hat was cocked jauntily on her long blonde hair and at her hip she wore her gun holster slung like a western gunslinger. And, as always, the evil-looking Doberman crouched near her, its tongue protruding from its dripping lips, as if too long for its ugly snout. As von Dodenburg, bathed and shaved for the first time in two months, approached, it raised its black head, fixed him with its baleful gaze and gave a low growl, as if wondering what a chunk of the stranger's leg might taste like on this cold frosty morning.

Without looking down, Grafin von Falkenstein flicked the black leather whip she carried in her black-gloved hand and snapped coldly, 'Enough, Bello! Whenever will you learn how to behave?' She smiled coldly at the SS officer. 'Discipline is the basis of our German culture, don't you think, *Obersturmbannführer*? I *love* discipline!' and she sighed for reasons known only to herself and gave him a knowing look.

Von Dodenburg made no reply. He had not yet quite got over the shock of discovering that *Colonel* von Falkenstein was a woman, and a damned attractive one at that. Her husband, the real *Oberst*, had been murdered, so she had told him the previous evening, by the Maquis three months before; and the way she had told it, his death was no great loss to the *Wehrmacht*.

Standing a little way off, Schulze, watching her firm buttocks rippling under the tight black material of her suit, nudged Matz and whispered, 'Phew! I'd sooner fuck a pair o' scissors than that one! She'd have the dick right off'n you, I'd bet!'

Matz, the expert, nodded in agreement, though there was

a disturbing thickening of his loins, as he watched the delightful arse. His worm was beginning to turn.

'This morning you said you wished to show me your, er, great surprise,' von Dodenburg said, as outside the hammering started once again and for the second time his nostrils caught the acrid smell of burning paint.

'Of course. Please follow me. Bello, you lazy dog, on your feet.' She jerked the metal chain cruelly and Bello started to his feet. He knew what discipline was all right.

'Do you think the hound fucks her?' Schulze asked as she strode majestically to the door, but Matz had no answer to that question. He was too concerned with that splendid butt and the fact that his 'worm' was very definitely 'turning'.

Von Dodenburg savoured the clean mountain air as they stood together at the head of the ancient steps looking down at the cobbled courtyard below. It was a hive of activity. Civilians in overalls, all of whom tipped their caps and bowed when they spotted the Countess, were hurrying back and forth. Oxy-acetylene welding torches flared purple. Metal was trundled back and forth on squeaking handcarts. An ox lumbered through the yard, twin streams of hot air spurting from its flared nostrils as it dragged a great piece of metal behind it over the cobbles. From all sides came the hollow clang of metal being beaten. It was more like a Ruhr factory than a rural castle hidden in this remote wilderness. 'Funny place to find a workshop, Countess,' he ventured.

'Exactly,' she answered in that cold, brittle manner of hers, 'that is why Schloss Falkenstein was selected by the *Reichsführer SS*.'

'Selected for what?'

She didn't seem to hear his question. Instead she said, 'The enemy has been in occupation for two months and has his spies everywhere' – she made a gesture of slitting a throat – 'though fortunately they didn't survive long. So the Americans suspect nothing of what goes on up here. Schloss Falkenstein is the ideal place for what Herr Himmler has in mind. But, please, let me show you what we produce.' She looked down at Bello who was not moving. Again she flicked the hound with her whip, snapping, 'Bello, you must learn discipline – soon. Or I'll have to beat it into you again!' Bello reached up and licked her gloved hand, as if overjoyed at the prospect.

Von Dodenburg gasped. The wooden shed which had been constructed along the whole length of the inner castle wall, facing the courtyard, so that from the air it would appear to be a stable or something of that sort, was packed with vehicles in various states of repair – and they were all American! Six-wheeled Staghound armoured cars, Sherman tanks, White halftracks, many jeeps, most of them bearing the scars of battle, holes gouged into the metal by anti-tank shells; reddened metal where the engines had caught fire and burnt away the olive-drab paint; shattered tracks lying behind the immobile tanks like severed limbs.

'Where in the devil's name did you get this lot?' von Dodenburg managed to stutter at last.

She smiled coldly, pleased with the little surprise she had managed to spring on him. 'The litter of our local battlefields. The American advance through the Vosges in September lasted two weeks. Our brave boys, hopelessly outnumbered as they were, made the enemy invader pay dearly for his temerity. Once the Americans were through, wasteful people that they are, they left their advance route littered with material. So we had our pick. At first, of course, it was difficult for my people. All we had was the peasants' ox-carts to move them. Once, however, we put one of their halftracks on the road, ready for towing, things became much much easier.'

'And fuel?' von Dodenburg asked, astonished by the amount of armour she and her 'peasants' had managed to drag to this remote place.

She shrugged carelessly and her small breasts, nipples jutting out like spikes with the cold, rose under the tight black material. 'Black market or ambushes. Their convoys are taken easily. They are not guarded and those black monkeys who drive their supply trucks are afraid of their own shadows. One shot and they surrender. Just like that!' She snapped her fingers and Bello crouched in fear, as if he expected to be beaten at any moment. She giggled. But there was no warmth in the sound.

'But what is it all for, *Grafin?*' he asked, still not recovered from his surprise. 'I mean why are you accumulating all this *Ami* armour. Your people can't drive those things and man their guns, can they?'

By way of an answer, she stabbed her finger at him, gave him one of her wintry smiles and said, 'Come, my dear Colonel, let us take a look at the view.'

Watching them walk towards the wall, Schulze said to Matz, 'I'll take that back about rather fucking a pair of scissors, Matzi. Willya cast yer glassy orbits on them flanks o' hers! Ger, I'd like to get my good honest German sausage inside them. I'd give her a poke she wouldn't soon forget!' He grabbed the bulging front of his trousers dramatically.

'Ner, *you* forget it,' Matz said sourly. 'She's strictly officer country. Reserved for colonels and above, that is, if she really does spread her legs like normal gash does. My only worry, Schulze, is where that pretty ass is gonna lead poor old Wotan.' He frowned. 'I don't like it, I don't like it one frigging bit, Schulzi.'

'Look!' she commanded, pointing over the ancient rampart to the snowbound countryside beyond. Obediently he followed the direction she indicated. A thousand metres below lay the great and fruitful Alsatian plain which stretched to the Rhine, hidden somewhere beyond the horizon. Here and there the snow was broken by dark patches which were farmhouses, or huddled settlements grouped around one of those typical onion-towered Baroque churches of the area. Below them a couple of tiny dark figures plodded stolidly through the snow behind their lumbering oxen; peasants heading for the next village, von Dodenburg guessed. It all looked very picturesque and peaceful, but he knew she hadn't brought him up here to admire the view. He waited, suddenly overcome by a feeling of unease, even apprehension.

'You know our beloved Führer's plans, do you?' she snapped suddenly.

'Plans?'

'Yes, plans,' she barked impatiently.

'All I know from the orders *Reichsführer* Himmler sent me is that I had to make it to Schloss Falkenstein where I was to place myself at the disposal of Colonel von Falkenstein. *You.* I thought it would be your job to see that we were smuggled through the *Ami* lines somehow or other and back to the Reich for rest and refitting . . .' He broke off, knowing even as he uttered the words that his previous fears had been well-founded. There would be no rest and refitting back in the Homeland if Grafin von Falkenstein had her way.

'Listen, *Obersturmbannführer* von Dodenburg,' she hissed, those icy-grey eyes of hers glittering fanatically, her breasts heaving with barely suppressed excitement. 'This is not the time for rest. This is the time for action! Our Führer needs only to gain a few months and then our deadly V-weapons* will wipe the enemy off the face of the earth. Then, at last, we shall have the final victory!'

Von Dodenburg was not impressed by her talk of V-weapons. The 'Poison Dwarf', as the Minister of Propaganda, Dr Goebbels was known, had been promising them to a hard-pressed German people for months now. But he *was* impressed by her fanaticism. There were few people back in the Reich who still believed so fervently in 'final victory' as she obviously did. He waited for her to continue. Down below in the courtyard Schulze spat on the icy cobbles and grunted. 'It don't look to me, comrade, as if we're gonna go home to mother this side of Christmas, 1944!' But for once 'Mrs Schulze's handsome son' was wrong.

---

* The secret German revenge weapons. V = '*Vergeltung*' (revenge)

'Soon,' she said, 'the Führer will strike back and give the Amis a taste of their own medicine. Once again Alsace will be German!' Her eyes sparkled and von Dodenburg could see that it was not just fanaticism that made them gleam. Grafin von Falkenstein was using something more potent than that to give her a 'high'. He noted the red patches around her nostrils and guessed, correctly, that Grafin von Falkenstein was a cocaine-addict.

'This is what the Führer plans,' she continued, overlooking the suddenly thoughtful look which had appeared on her listener's face. 'Soon – we don't know exactly when – the Führer intends to launch a great double offensive in the West. First he will attack in the Belgium Ardennes. Then, when the enemy begins to deploy whatever reserves he has here in Alsace to the north, the second blow will strike them.' Swiftly and accurately she sketched in Hitler's bold plan for the defeat of the Anglo-Americans in the West while von Dodenburg listened in silence, his horror and disbelief growing by the instant. It wasn't possible, *it couldn't be possible*, that after the catastrophic defeats of the summer, Germany could ever again launch an offensive! But, drugged and fanatical as she was, Grafin von Falkenstein made it quite clear that the Reich *was* striking back; and he had a sinking feeling that SS Assault Regiment Wotan, battered as it was, had some role to play in this new offensive.

'Thus there will be two great pincers surging through Alsace, one from the north and one from the south, to converge to the west of Strasbourg and thus cut off the Franco-American armies here and ensure that our beloved Strasbourg is once again German!' She paused, eyes gleaming, bosom heaving with the effort of so much talking.

Bello growled and rattled the heavy metal chain attached to his collar, as if he too could not wait for the great day to commence.

She paused for breath and continued. 'There is only one problem. Even when the *Amis* draw away their reserves to fight in the north, our High Command is confident that they will leave one regiment of their 36th Infantry Division behind – some three thousand men in all – down there in Haguenau.' She pointed to the vague outline of a town to the east, a smudge on the horizon. 'There will remain the only sizeable force of enemy soldiers behind the Rhine front.'

Von Dodenburg nodded and admitted to himself that, drugs or not, Grafin von Falkenstein was a very determined woman; she would have made a good soldier.

'Now, Haguenau is vitally important to the success of the Alsatian operation, *Obersturmbannführer*. The pincer coming north from the Colmar Pocket must pass through the Lower Vosges if it is going to link up successfully with the one coming from the Reich. A determined defence of Haguenau might well have serious consequences.'

'I see,' von Dodenburg said, though he didn't really. What had all this got to do with him and his men? He felt a sense of anger rising within him. Did she know what he and his men had been through these last terrible months? How could she talk so enthusiastically about new offensives and 'final victory'? What the devil did *she* know of the horrors of real war? 'And what role is my regiment – what is left of it – supposed to play in this great plan?' he asked. But irony was wasted on the Countess.

'I am glad you ask, *Obersturmbannführer*, I am surprised you didn't earlier,' she said as if his weary men were only too eager to die for 'Folk, Fatherland and Führer'. 'We – *you* – have to take that *Ami* garrison in Haguenau by surprise in the first hour of the attack. I have a thousand loyal peasants under my command. Brave, willing and armed, but untrained.' She flashed him a hard look and he could see that she could hardly contain her excitement at what was to come. 'Your men should be able to train them in time. It should only take a matter of a few days, don't you think?'

'Oh yes,' he replied cynically, 'only a matter of a few days to turn peasants into soldiers.'

But his cynicism was wasted on her. 'On the day my people will effectively sabotage every *Ami* installation in the town.

Roads, railways, radio station – we will take over the lot
before the *Amis* know what is happening to them. Haguenau
is loyal to our cause anyway. Its citizens will occasion us no
trouble.'

'And Wotan?'

'It will take the *Ami* garrison.'

He stared at her incredulously. 'Do you really believe what
you are saying?' he said in amazement. '*Two hundred men
dealing with three thousand well-armed infantrymen?*'

She laughed a little hysterically and pressed his arm. He
could feel the electric excitement exuding from her body.
There was something almost sexual about it. 'You are
forgetting the armour, my dear von Dodenburg,' she gushed.
'In those sheds we have ten Shermans, half-a-dozen halftracks and three armoured cars, plus one armoured flame-
throwing halftrack! A very potent force indeed. Think of it,
Obersturmbannführer. The *Amis* wake up on the morning of the
great day to find what they think is one of their armoured
columns advancing on their barracks. What do you think will
happen, eh?' She stared up at him, eyes sparkling feverishly
like those of a crazy woman.

Von Dodenburg whistled softly, impressed in spite of his
reservations. 'So that's it, eh? SS Assault Regiment Wotan is
going to play the Trojan Horse.'

CHAPTER 3

The rattle of musketry, dampened by the thin grey fog which curled in and out of the snow-heavy firs which bordered both sides of the forest track, was faint but definite. There was no mistake about that. Even with the Weasels' engines running they could hear it.

Colonel Petersen, his face pinched with the freezing cold, cocked his head to one side and let the breeze carry the noise to him. It was definitely controlled fire, volley after volley of it. He looked at Wolf, muffled up to his GI glasses against the biting cold, and said, 'Now what the Sam Hill do you make of that, Captain?'

Wolf took off his glasses which had steamed up instantly he had left the vehicle and wiped them with the end of his khaki scarf. 'Well, sir, for my money, it sounds to me like a range, a small-arms range.'

'Exactly! That's what I thought, too. But what in tarnation is a range doing up here, eh? Neither we nor the frogs have troops this high, do we?'

'No, sir,' Wolf replied dutifully, his brain racing. 'The nearest US troops are on the other side of the mountains. The Thirty-Sixth are based at Haguenau.'

'Then who in God's name is out in this wilderness firing?' Colonel Petersen demanded, exasperated.

Wolf didn't answer, but the look on his sharp little face told the Colonel all he needed to know. '*Them?*'

'Yes sir. It can only be the SS.'

'But they are veterans, trained soldiers,' Petersen objected. 'What would they be doing firing their pieces on a range?'

Wolf shrugged. 'There's only one way to find out, sir,' he said.

Petersen nodded. 'You're right as always, Wolf. Let's roll 'em.'

'Sir,' Wolf caught him by the arm and lowered his voice so

that the nearest Weasel driver couldn't hear him. 'If it is the SS up there and we have to go into action against them, we'll leave the vehicles of course?'

'Of course. When the crunch comes your infantryman has got to get on to his two flat feet and attack. Why do you ask?'

'The drivers, sir.' Wolf looked at Big Red, but his sullen unshaven face revealed nothing of what he was thinking. 'I don't trust them as far as I can throw them which is not far. Given half a chance they'll bug out on us.'

Petersen nodded. 'What do you suggest?'

'This, sir. Your Master-Sergeant Lee looks to me a top-class noncom. I don't think he'd take much crap from the drivers, even if they are southern rednecks.'

Petersen smiled. 'No, Master-Sergeant Lee is not exactly Caspar Milquetoast. Sometimes I'm a little afraid of him myself.'

'Well, sir, what about leaving a platoon under his command to guard the vehicles?' He winked. 'In fact, they'll be guarding Big Red and his hoodlums.'

'Excellent, excellent! Without those vehicles we're sunk. I'll see to it straight away.'

Five minutes later they were rolling once more, heading straight for the sound of the firing. Petersen's 'Fighting Coons' were about to begin their date with destiny, while up in the leading Weasel Big Red's mind raced as he considered just how he was going to shaft these uppity niggers once and for all.

A mere three kilometres away Schulze eyed the peasants lying on the sacks in the snow with a jaundiced eye. A young SS corporal was explaining to them how to fire rapid bursts with adjustments in order to cover a given area. Most of them stared up at him with their moonlike faces as if he were speaking a foreign language, instead of German.

'Just look at 'em,' he said scornfully, 'for most of them a rifle is as much use as a pecker'd be for the Pope!'

Matz nodded in agreement. 'Bunch o' cardboard soldiers, real Christmas tree decorations,' he agreed sourly. 'Someone must have shat in the C.O.'s brain to have made him believe he could make soldiers outa this bunch of farmyard shite-shovellers. I reckon . . .'

But the rest of his words were drowned by a ragged volley as the Alsatians fired at the bales of straw, crudely painted up as range targets. Most of them missed by metres and the two veterans watched contemptuously as the 'wides' sliced up the snow all about the targets.

'Shit on the shingle!' Schulze exclaimed. 'That bunch of wettails, couldn't hit a barn door, even if you ordered 'em to charge it with their bayonets!'

'Yer,' Matz agreed. 'But what are we training them yokels for, that's what I'd like to frigging well know?' He frowned, suddenly gloomy, as the wisps of fog curled about the make-shift range like a silent grey cat. 'What has that bunch o' piss pansies got to do with Wotan, eh, Schulze?'

'You might well ask, little arse-with-ears!' Schulze agreed, sombre too. 'I know the C.O. doesn't like it, whatever it is. You can see it written all over his face. Wotan has been taking its knocks for too frigging long and all the C.O. wants is to get us back home. So why are we farting around *here*?'

Matz tapped the end of his red nose significantly, as the corporal ordered the Alsatian yokels to reload. 'It's that piece of aristocratic gash with her frigging Bello. She's got him by the ball-race somehow or other, mark my words.'

'But she's only a frigging civvie, and a half-frog at that,' Schulze began to object at the same instant as there was a sudden burst of rapid fire.

'*Who told you buggers to . . .*' the young corporal started to yell as a series of bubbling pink holes were stitched across the front of his tunic. He stared down at them, as if he couldn't believe this was happening to *him*. A quick succession of emotions flashed across his face – anger, surprise, sorrow, pain, agony. He pitched forward into the snow, dead before he hit the ground. For a moment the two old comrades were rooted to the spot, unable to react. Suddenly Schulze let out a tremendous yell, bellowing out orders, unslinging his Schmeisser as a long line of cautious, khaki-clad figures began to emerge from the forest, firing as they came.

'Holy strawsack!' Matz cried. '*It's the frigging Amis!*'

'An absolute weakling!' Grafin von Falkenstein sneered, as she pointed at the oil painting of her late husband above the great open fireplace with her black leather whip. 'Weak through and through.'

At her feet Bello growled, as if he too were contemptuous of the late Graf.

Only half-interested, von Dodenburg stared at the man, posing in the black peacetime SS uniform, a scattering of decorations on his chest, hand on his hip almost mincingly. There was something decadent and sickly about the dead man, with his sallow face and receding chin. 'I see your late husband was in Russia,' he said for the sake of saying something. 'I note he wears the Order of the Frozen Meat*,' he added using the old soldier's slang term for the medal.

She was not amused at the expression, but von Dodenburg had already realized that Grafin von Falkenstein had absolutely no sense of humour. 'I had to force him to go, went down on my knees to plead with him to volunteer for the honour of the von Falkensteins and that of my own family, the von Gottas. My God, how he tried to worm his way out of it! He almost wept. But I was firm, very firm.' She swished her black whip and Bello jumped with surprise. 'There was a need for sacrifice, even the supreme one, if necessary. Strangely enough, he survived eleven months out there, only to have his throat cut in Alsace last summer by some unwashed pimp from Marseilles masquerading as a resistance soldier.' She looked at her nails, seemingly bored by the

---

* Medal given to soldiers who had suffered frostbite during the campaign in Russia

whole messy business. Von Dodenburg looked at the painted nails, long, bright red, and cruel, and thought that they looked as if they had just been dipped in blood.

She forgot her late husband and, turning to von Dodenburg, stared at him hard. Von Dodenburg felt embarrassed. He hadn't had a woman since after Cassino the previous June and this one was looking at him as if she were mentally stripping him naked.

'You would be good to *breed* from!' she breathed, eyes narrowed to slits, the pupils reduced to mere pinpoints; and he knew why. As he had been about to enter her room, he had seen her sniffing the white powder up each nostril through the bejewelled tube she used to inhale the cocaine. She was high again.

'You are the kind of Aryan, *Reichsführer SS* Himmler dreams about. Tall, blond, blue-eyed – *vigorous!*' she emphasized the word, looking at him challengingly.

In spite of himself von Dodenburg felt the old familiar stirring in his loins. His breath was coming a little faster as he realized that he desired Grafin von Falkenstein, crazy and as doped as she was. He swallowed hard and licked his lips, which were suddenly very dry.

What happened next seemed to him later to be the stuff that nightmares are made of – a heady mixture of horror and bizarre comedy, totally lacking in logic and reality. Suddenly (how, he never managed to figure out afterwards) he was drinking brandy after brandy, while she was sniffing the deadly white powder from her bejewelled tube, snorting like an angry bull as she did so, her breath coming in short gasps.

Then she was naked, a long white body, the body hair shaven so that her plump sex seemed to pout. Her eyes glittered as she ripped at his uniform, muttering impossible obscenities that would have frightened him if he had not been so sexually excited and rather drunk.

'I know what you want, you swine,' she shrieked, her small

sharp-pointed breasts heaving wildly, '*you want to blindfold me*
. . . tie me down against my will. . . . There is nothing a weak little
woman like I can do against your savage strength, you pigdog. . . .
You will use your brute force to rip open my legs and have your filthy
way with me. . . . You want to thrust that monstrous thing you have
hanging there into me, savaging me with it, ripping me in two,
ravishing me in spite of my pleas for mercy, my cries for help. . . . Oh
. . . oh . . . oh!' Her pale white body writhed as if she were in
the throes of a fit, her sex surging up and down as if she could
not wait to suffer that awful fate.

All this time von Dodenburg was trying, with little success,
it must be said, to kiss her small breasts and fondle her firm
hard. stomach. But the damned woman couldn't, *wouldn't*,
keep still, and the constant flow of obscenities frightened him
not a little.

'*I know you male swine, you'll beat me first. . . . I know you'll*
whip me!' she cried through gritted teeth, her eyes closed. '*Till*
the blood flows, so that I'll submit to your filthy lusts.' Eyes still
screwed shut, she kicked the little dog whip in his direction.
'*Of course, you'll want to blindfold and gag me with that filthy shirt of*
yours . . . Oh, quick, quick, wrap it around my head and pull it tight. I
do hope it stinks of male sweat.'

Hardly knowing what he was doing, the room swaying
before his eyes, he tied the shirt around her face, as she
mumbled, '*Tight, for God's sake, tie it tighter . . . and now the*
whip. . . . I MUST BE DISCIPLINED.'

It was thus that the old butler found them as he opened the
door when his knock remained unanswered – a tense,
quivering, naked countess with a male shirt tightly wrapped
round her head, and, facing her, *Obersturmbannführer* von
Dodenburg, his trousers round his ankles, holding Bello's whip
in his hand, looking exceedingly bewildered and with no sign
of the necessary physical transformation that is customary in
situations of this kind. The butler cleared his throat politely
and said, 'I thought it was my duty to inform the lady and

gentleman that firing has been reported further down the valley. I hope, madam, I have not entered at an inopportune moment?'

Gasping for breath, face sweat-covered and flushed scarlet, but with her eyes normal again, the Countess removed von Dodenburg's shirt and said with a wave of her hand, all *noblesse oblige* now, 'No, you acted quite correctly, Johann. Thank you for your courtesy. You may go.'

Johann gave a stiff bow, his ancient limbs creaking as he did so, and backed out to the door, closing it softly behind him.

Von Dodenburg staggered to the window and somehow managed to wrench it open. The room was filled with ice-cold air. He shivered and sucked in great gulps. He felt his head beginning to clear. Below, the snowbound countryside was still shrouded in fog. He could see only a couple of hundred metres, but there was no doubt about it. There was no missing the angry snap-and-crackle of small-arms fire. There was a fire fight going on down there.

He swayed back into the centre of the room. Already Grafin von Falkenstein was slipping into her clothes, while Bello growled at the door as if impatient to be off. She flashed him one of those icy looks of hers, as if nothing had happened, and for a moment von Dodenburg thought he must have been dreaming. Was this the same woman who only minutes ago had been writhing naked on the rug, with his shirt tied around her head, crying the filthiest of obscenities and begging him to 'ravish' her? It did not seem possible!

She buckled her pistol belt around her waist and said, 'Whoever they are they must be wiped out, *Obersturmbannführer*.'

'Yes, wiped out,' he echoed stupidly as he fumbled with his boots, his head still spinning.

'*Jawohl*,' she snapped. 'No mercy must be shown. They must be liquidated. Every single one of them. None of them must escape to report what is going on up here. The future of German-Alsace depends upon it. *Wipe them out!*' Her eyes blazed and then she was gone, striding out of the door, Bello trotting behind her.

CHAPTER 4

'All right, titty-suckers!' Schulze growled to the survivors as they crouched in the snowy ditch, the Americans now gone to ground some three hundred metres further down the slope, 'listen to what we're gonna do!' A slug howled off the rock to his right, splattering his face with tiny particles of splintered rock and snow. Schulze wiped his face with his big hand, as if he might have been swatting away an importuning fly, while the awed Alsatians watched, wondering how he could be so cool under fire. 'Me and Corporal Matz is gonna try to get back to the castle and bring up reinforcements. You lot o' cardboard soldiers are gonna hold them for as long as yer can.'

'But if they charge us, Sergeant-Major,' one of the scared peasants asked, 'what are we supposed to do then?'

'What do you think, yokel? You frigging well surrender, toot-sweet, that's what you do. Unless you want to make a frigging corpse.' He wasted no more time on the peasants. 'You ready, you little cripple?' he demanded of Matz.

By way of an answer Matz stuck up his middle finger and growled, 'Try that for size, you big shiteheel.'

'Can't!' Schulze answered. 'Got a double-decker bus up there already. You,' he turned to the man at the far end of the ditch. 'Put yer cap on the end of your piece and raise it up above the ditch when I say now.' Obediently the man prepared to do as Schulze ordered. 'Grenade,' Schulze snapped at Matz. 'Move it!'

Matz whipped his second grenade out of his boot and tossed it carelessly to his friend who caught it. He pulled out the china pin. Matz did the same. The two of them tensed, while the peasants watched in dull stupidity.

'*Now*!' Schulze yelled.

Things then happened fast. The yokel raised his rifle with

the cap on the end. A burst of American machine-gun fire shattered the butt. The cap flew off and the yokel yelped with the shock to his arm and reeled back. Matz and Schulze popped up. As one they threw their grenades. With a roar they exploded a hundred metres away, sending up two mushrooms of smoke, snow and rock. In a flash, the two of them were out of the ditch and pelting frantically for the summit. The Americans below spotted them immediately. But those two grenades had put them off their aim. Slugs cut the air all around them. Arms working like pistons, the two men zig-zagged, Matz going all out in spite of his wooden leg. Schulze yelled as a bullet went through his tunic and scored his arm.

'Ain't frigging fair,' he gasped, 'Shooting at a feller when he's got his back turned!'

Next to him Matz yelled wildly, carried away by the crazy exuberance of combat, *'Follow me, the captain's got a hole in his ass!'*

The next moment they were diving over the ridge into a bank of deep snow, laughing and gasping like two crazy schoolboys, while down below Colonel Petersen lowered his glasses and said to Wolf, 'All right, no more pussy-footing, don't you think? The SS have abandoned the civvies. Those two'll lead us to the main party. Whistle up the Weasels. The civvies can stay there till hell boils over, as far as I'm concerned. Let's root hog and catch up with those SS jerks!'

Wolf took a deep breath and blew three shrill blasts on his whistle. It was the signal for Master-Sergeant Lee, in charge of the vehicles down below beyond the trees, to bring up the Weasels.

The shrill blast of the whistle caught Master-Sergeant Lee by surprise, although he had been waiting for it all the time. He had objected strongly to the task the Colonel had allotted him. He had not volunteered for the infantry to guard a

bunch of nigger-hating rednecks when the rest of the
battalion was going into action. But he realized that the task
showed Colonel Petersen's trust in him. He had just gone over
the ridge to take a leak (he had not wanted to urinate in front
of the rednecks; he knew what *they* thought about 'nigger
dicks'. And he wouldn't give them the opportunity to make
the kind of snide remarks their type always made on such
occasions.) When in the middle of it all, just as he was
directing a stream of steaming yellow urine against the
nearest rock, the signal came. He stuffed his organ back into
his pants and buttoned up his flies with frozen fingers that felt
like clumsy sausages. Slinging his carbine over his shoulder,
he set off at an awkward trot towards the spot where his squad
'guarded' the Weasels. But in his haste he failed to see the
patch of slick ice beneath the thin layer of snow. Suddenly his
feet were sliding beneath him and he was down. Somehow his
carbine jerked loose from his shoulder. '*Shoot!*' he cursed in
the same instant that the butt whipped up and struck him a
sickening blow in the small of the back. He shot forward
helplessly. Next instant his helmeted head connected with a
rock and he blacked out at the very moment that that first
angry burst of machine-gun fire erupted from the cab of Big
Red's Weasel.

'*Okay, okay,*' Big Red bellowed over the vicious chatter of the
.5 inch machine gun which they had stolen from the niggers
the previous evening. 'You've got the black bastards. *Don't
waste no more fuckin' ammo on them!*'
    The sweating gunner relaxed his finger on the trigger and
the firing ceased, followed for a few moments by an echoing
silence, broken only by the moans of the wounded and dying.
They had caught the niggers completely by surprise. At the
same moment that the whistle had sounded and they had
turned to the west to see what the reason for the signal was,
'Hambone' Perkins had whipped the m.g. from beneath the
tarpaulin in the second Weasel and opened fire. It had been a

massacre. The niggers hadn't had a chance. The moment they had started to unsling their weapons, that first salvo had blasted them apart. Then they had been galvanized into crazy, frenetic puppets, their limbs flailing, high-pitched screams coming from their gaping mouths, black faces all fear and wide yellow eyes, as the slugs ripped into them. At that range even 'Hambone' couldn't miss. Laughing crazily, enjoying every second of the merciless slaughter, he had slewed the weapon from left to right, mowing them down mercilessly until Big Red's cry had somehow penetrated through to his brain and he had relaxed his finger on the gun's trigger.

Big Red licked his lips in triumph, ears deaf to the pleading of one of the wounded niggers who was crying piteously for his mother, '*Mammy, where is you, Mammy. . . ?*' Over and over again.

'Now we've shown the nigger trash, haven't we, guys?' He rubbed his hands up and down his bulging flies, as if the sight of the dead and dying black soldiers lying there in the snow gave him actual sexual pleasure. 'Better than any nigger lynching back home any day.'

There was a murmur of agreement from his comrades and someone cried, 'Hell, Big Red, when we go back to Dixie all of us ought to take one of them there popguns with us! *Then we'd really clear out that nigger trash* for good!'

There was a burst of coarse male laughter at the thought, but then someone said, and there was no mistaking the fear in his voice, 'But what if the Army finds out, Big Red? I mean they're only niggers and don't amount to nothing. Still the Inspector General . . .'

'Nobody's gonna talk, Joe,' Big Red interrupted the speaker.

'But they ain't all dead. What about them wounded niggers? They could talk, couldn't they?'

'Sure,' Big Red answered easily. '*If* they survived, they could. But they ain't gonna survive, are they? What do they say? Dead men tell no tales.'

'But even if we do croak 'em, Big Red,' the soldier

protested, 'they could get to know we did it.'

Big Red reached into his combat boot and pulled out an SS dagger, with its imitation ivory handle decorated with the swastika. He had bought it off a guy in the Third Infantry for five dollars outside Nancy. He had intended to send it to his old woman as a kind of warning. No fooling around with those jerks who worked at the local defence plant. She wasn't collecting no ten thousand dollars for him.* He was coming home and, if he found out she'd been playing the field while he had been overseas, he'd do a little fancy nigger-carving on her pretty face.

He raised the SS dagger so that they could all see it. 'So,' he said, 'let the frigging Inspector General do his frigging inspecting. All he'll find is that the Kraut SS did for our poor black soldiers.' He spat into the snow and they laughed, telling each other that Big Red was a real smart hombre. They'd never catch him with his skivvies down.

Slowly Big Red ran the razor-sharp blade across his palm, savouring the feel of the steel almost lovingly. 'Now I'm gonna show you guys what we do with niggers back home where I come from. No messing with the black filth there, I swear.' He strode over to where the black bodies lay stacked like logs where they had been mown down so treacherously. The others followed him over the snow, now coloured dark red by pools of blood. Like spectators at some sport or other, they watched avidly as Big Red began to move from body to body, occasionally giving one a kick in order to ascertain whether it was still alive or not. But in vain. Negro after negro was already dead. Then the boy who had called for his mother began to cry again.

Big Red's piglike little eyes lit up. 'There's one of the cock-suckers, boys,' he shouted joyfully.

'What ya gonna do, Big Red?' the one called Hambone cried. 'Saw off his black dick?'

Big Red shook his head. 'No, sir. Them Krauts ain't red-

* GIs overseas were insured for 10,000 dollars in case they were killed

blooded like us. They don't go in for that good ole back-home stuff. We want the brass to think we was attacked by the SS and bugged out in an attempt to save the vehicles.' He chuckled. 'Hell, fellahs, I do believe we'll all get the Bronze Star for this in the end.' He nodded to the two men next to him. 'Get a hold o' that darkie, willya?'

Obediently they took hold of the wounded soldier, blood jetting from his nearly severed arm. That burst of m.g. fire had ripped it apart and shattered the bone. Suddenly his eyes flickered open and the look of pain was replaced by one of hope as he recognized the uniform. 'Help me, Corporal!' he gasped, his chest heaving. 'I got hit bad.' The pain of his shattered arm was too much and his face was contorted in agony.

'Sure, sure,' Big Red said. 'I'm gonna help you, son. I'll soon put you out of yer pain.'

The others sniggered knowingly.

'Hold him tight,' he ordered as he raised the razor-sharp dagger. He placed the point against the youth's Adam's apple. The boy stared up at him, his eyes filled with fear and bewilderment. 'What are ya gonna do, Corporal?' he asked, voice almost out of control.

'Just gonna put ya out of ya pain, nigger – *for good*!' Big Red hesitated no longer, but drove the dagger home, straight into the youth's throat. '*Die, nigger*!' he grunted.

The youth gave a scream which was cut off almost at once. His spine arched as tense as a drawn bow. The other two held onto his writhing body as Big Red calmly worked the dagger round, widening the wound, seemingly oblivious to the blood pouring from it, as he sawed through the jugular vein.

The boy went limp. Only one last faint whisper. Almost gently, his black head lolled to one side. He was dead. Big Red let go of the dagger, wiped his hands on the dead youth's uniform and got to his feet, staring down at his victim like a butcher might do at some steer he had slaughtered, pleased with his handiwork. The others were silent and a brooding stillness fell over that place of death.

Big Red laughed callously. 'Come on, fellahs, let's get out of this hell-hole and back down to civilization.' Sullenly, their mood depressed for some reason they could not quite explain, the drivers walked back to their vehicles. Big Red waited a moment longer, staring at the dead negroes piled up like offal outside a butcher's shop. Then he placed his hand at the rim of his helmet liner and grinned. 'So long niggers. *Your country salutes you*!' And with that he was gone, to die just as sordidly in a Paris whorehouse brawl three months later.

The roar of the Weasels' motors starting up roused Master-Sergeant Lee from the black pit of unconsciousness. He shook his head – and wished he hadn't. Tenderly he felt the back of his neck, red and silver stars exploding before his eyes. There was one hell of a bump there. It all came back to him in a rush. Groggily, he staggered to his feet, trying to focus his eyes, and broke into a lurching trot, swaying from side to side as if he were drunk. There had been the signal and somehow he had knocked himself out. Now the Weasels had gone – without him! Christ on a crutch, what would the Colonel think of him? That he was yellow? Sick and nauseated as he was, he forced himself up the knee-deep snow of the slope beyond the place where they had parked the vehicles, crying as he stumbled upwards, 'Don't go without me, guys. Wait for good ole Sergeant Lee. Don't let me down, fellahs . . .' The words froze on his lips and he stumbled to a stop on the brow of the hill. There they were, all dead, every single one of them. His handsome black face suddenly contorted with almost unbearable grief. The white bastards had somehow surprised them and shot them in cold blood. It had been a cruel massacre.

For what seemed an age (later he could never work out whether it had been hours or merely minutes) he stood there on the ridge, shoulders bowed, frozen tears trickling down his grief-stricken face, as he stared down at their dead young faces. Their eyes seemed to gaze up at him as if in silent reproach. Why had he gone to take a leak? Why had he left them to be tricked by those murdering rednecks? Why, why, *why*?

But Master-Sergeant Lee could find no answer to those questions and to his dying day (he would relive that terrible scene virtually every night of his life before he went to sleep) he never would. He, the professional, the guy who knew all the angles, had failed them; and he had survived while they were dead, slaughtered so cruelly and so young.

Finally he turned. Later he would come back with a squad to bury them before the wild animals found their bodies, but now he knew he had to inform the Colonel. How he was going to explain it, he didn't know. If he was lucky, perhaps some Kraut bullet would put an end to him, but first the Colonel must know that Petersen's Fighting Coons were without their wheels, and if they didn't secure their objective soon, they might well die in the open in these freezing mountains.

Sobbing bitterly, Master-Sergeant Lee broke into a shambling trot. Behind him the corpses started to stiffen in the cold. Slowly, gently, flakes of fresh snow began to drift down to cover their dead faces.

CHAPTER 5

The soft hum suddenly became an ear-splitting howl. Von Dodenburg, sober and fully alert once more, cupped his hands about his mouth and bellowed urgently. 'Take cover! Hit the dirt, everybody! *Incoming mail!*' The *Amis* had found them again!

His veterans dropped as one. The Alsatian civilians were slower and for a moment they stared up at the sky from where this strange banshee-like howl was coming, bewilderment written on their faces.

'*Down, yokels,*' von Dodenburg shrieked as the deadly black steel eggs began to fall from the sky. Too late!

The first salvo of enemy mortar bombs ran the length of the courtyard and in an instant they were all engulfed in hot smoke. The earth heaved and quaked. Red-hot, razor-sharp shards of metal flew everywhere. The Alsatians went down on all sides, screaming and shrieking as the shrapnel tore lumps of flesh from their helpless bodies.

Von Dodenburg kept his head down, ignoring the cries of the wounded Alsatians who were strewn on both sides. He caught a glimpse of a farm youth, both legs severed, trying to totter forward on his bloody stumps. Then the next salvo from the American mortars dug in on the opposite hill engulfed him and he cringed, his head tucked in both hands, waiting for the first blow to strike him.

Scarlet flame erupted on all sides. More screams. He coughed and sneezed, his lungs were choked by the acrid fumes of the explosives. For a moment he lay there paralysed with fear, blinded by smoke, unable to move. Then a familiar coarse voice bored into his consciousness as Schulze roared, 'Frigging balls o' flying shit! *That salvo whipped away me duds!*'

Von Dodenburg blinked. Matz was staggering about,

face blackened with smoke and glistening with sweat, pointing to his mouth, unable to speak, whether with the effort of having run so far or with laughter at Schulze's predicament, von Dodenburg did not know nor much care at that moment. By his side Schulze was looking down at his big body in total amazement. Which wasn't surprising, for he was totally naked save for his boots and his helmet! The blast from that last salvo had ripped every stitch of clothing from his enormous body, leaving him apparently totally unharmed.

But von Dodenburg had no time to ponder the matter. He sprang to his feet, ignoring the dead and dying, and cried, 'Report!'

'Just over the hillside, sir,' Matz cried somewhat shakily, trying to spring to attention, but not succeeding very well. 'A whole battalion of them is my guess, and as black as the ace o' spades, the lot of them!'

Von Dodenburg dismissed the enemy soldiers' colour; there were too many other things to do. 'All right, Matz, rally the men. Get them down there into position. At the double. *Los, los!*'

Matz took one last look at the bewildered and embarrassed Schulze and shook his head, as if he could not understand the world any more, before limping off to carry out the C.O.'s orders.

'And me, sir?' Schulze asked plaintively. Suddenly von Dodenburg realized the absurdity of Schulze's position and fought back his laughter just in time, though he had never felt less like laughing. 'Well, if you want to fornicate, Schulze, you're wearing the right kind of uniform, I guess. But as our friends across the valley seem to have other things in mind, you'd better go into the Schloss and find yourself some clothes.'

Then von Dodenburg was gone, bellowing out orders to the dumbfounded Alsatians as he ran across the body-littered courtyard, leaving Schulze standing there muttering grimly that he'd rather 'fuck than fight'.

Five minutes later von Dodenburg watched the Americans

preparing for their attack on the castle, while Matz worked feverishly to settle in the defenders. Their tactics were unoriginal but sound, he thought to himself, as he watched the brown-clad figures through his binoculars, ducking instinctively as yet another mortar bomb whizzed over his head and thudded into the ground. They were trying to pin the defenders down with the mortar barrage from the hill opposite, while they worked a company round each flank, obviously hoping to surprise the defence from the rear. All very predictable, but it would work. They had nothing in the way of artillery, not even heavy machine guns capable of knocking out the *Ami* mortar teams who were out of range of the weapons available. Soon, he guessed, reasoning that the *Amis* were going to do everything by the book, they would throw in a feint to their front with the third company before attacking on the flanks. If one of those flank attacks looked like succeeding, the *Ami* battalion commander would throw in his reserve battalion to support it; and with the handful of Wotan troopers at his disposal, and the rabble of Alsatian civilians, he could never defend the whole perimeter of the castle effectively. Von Dodenburg lowered his glasses and sat back on his heels, his handsome face thoughtful.

From across the valley, muted by the softly falling snowflakes, there came the shrilling of whistles and the commands of officers and NCOs. The *Amis* were preparing for the feint attack.

Von Dodenburg considered. He knew he could beat off the initial attacks, even though he was greatly outnumbered. Indeed, he might well be able to hold the castle for a day, even two or three, if he could manage to switch his troops from one danger spot to another quickly enough. But he knew too that once the weather cleared he would be sunk within an hour. The *Amis* would rustle up their dive-bombers and *jabos*, and that would be the end of Wotan. The only way he could save his young men, what was left of them, was to clear out of Schloss Falkenstein. But he couldn't do that in daylight. Besides there was Himmler's order. '*Damn his order*!' a little

voice at the back of his mind said. 'Your first duty, Kuno, is to
SS Assault Regiment Wotan!'

He ducked as yet another salvo of mortar bombs slammed
into the earth around the castle, filling the air with shrapnel.
One of his troopers screamed out. Von Dodenburg risked a
glance. The back of the trooper's head had been sliced away
and he lay on his face, dying. What looked like a mess of grey
maggots was seeping from the gaping wound. The sight made
up von Dodenburg's mind for him. He would stop the
attack before it really started, to put the *Amis* off their stroke
and win a little precious time.

'You, you and you!' he called to the nearest troopers,
'follow me and keep your turnips down!'

The troopers rose from their holes as von Dodenburg set
off at a run back up the slope towards the castle. Almost
immediately an American machine-gunner spotted them
and the slow tick-tack of a heavy m.g. sounded across the
valley, like some irate woodpecker at work on a stubborn tree.
Slugs cut the air all around and a burst erupted the length of
the castle wall, sending little bits of stone and century-old dirt
spurting upwards. Von Dodenburg shook his head violently,
as if he were trying to shake off mosquitoes. Behind him one of
the troopers yelled and came to a sudden stop. He groaned
and sank to his knees in the snow.

'Don't stop!' von Dodenburg yelled urgently. 'Don't stop.
Someone'll look after him!'

They dashed for the cover of the entrance, slamming
against the inner wall as another burst missed them by
millimetres. For a moment they simply remained there, rib-
cages heaving hectically as if their lungs might well burst out
of them at any moment. Then, wordlessly, von Dodenburg
gave them the signal to follow him. Hurriedly they ran down
the corridor which was littered with shattered furniture and
old family portraits now full of bullet holes or ripped to shreds
by the mortar bombs. Von Dodenburg stepped over the dead
butler, who lay with not a mark on him, as if he were just
having a brief rest and would recommence his duties at

any moment. He pushed on out into the comparative safety of the courtyard.

It was packed with panic-stricken Alsatians, milling around, shouting and crying in their thick guttural dialect, or crouching behind pathetic wooden handcarts, which wouldn't stop the smallest piece of shrapnel.

Von Dodenburg wasted no time. 'You, you, and you!' he detailed them off, while his troopers emphasized his commands by jerking up their machine pistols threateningly. 'Into the shed. At the double, now. I want that flame-throwing half-track pushed out at once!'

Von Dodenburg prayed fervently that the halftrack's engine would start in this freezing cold weather. If it didn't, Wotan was sunk.

'*Stillgestanden*!' Grafin von Falkenstein barked like some kind of drill instructor back in the Reich.

Schulze, still naked save for his boots and the helmet which he now held protectively in front of his genitals, stared at the tall, imperious aristocrat, as if she were mad, which, in a way, she was, though poor Schulze did not yet know that.

'What did you say, madame?' he stuttered, feeling an awful fool.

'Don't you come to attention, Sergeant,' she demanded coldly, slapping her booted leg with her dog whip, 'when you are in the presence of a superior officer?' By her side Bello growled at the naked noncom.

'Superior officer? Attention?' Schulze asked, completely bewildered.

'No more talk, or it will be the worse for you, Sergeant,' she snapped. 'Put your helmet on, as regulations prescribe, and report yourself correctly to Oberst von Falkenstein!' Again she slapped her boot. 'Or it will be the worse for you, I promise you that.'

Wishing the earth would open up and swallow him, Schulze slowly placed his helmet on his cropped head and tried to come to the position of attention. Weakly, he called out the prescribed formula, '*Oberscharführer Schulze meldet sich zur Stelle!*'

Her cruel mouth dropped open as she saw what the big noncom had been hiding behind his steel helmet, and her eyes sparkled even more. She swayed, as if she might well faint, but managed to catch herself in time. 'Well done, Sergeant Schulze, well done!' she said in a husky voice. 'But we can't have you standing around like that. Follow me.'

'*Follow you?*' he echoed, hardly recognizing his own voice.

'Yes, to my boudoir.' She flung the words over her shoulder as she strode forward, suddenly in a great hurry. 'I still have the uniforms of the late Count there, and,' she added somewhat obscurely, 'his spurs naturally. You'll have to wear his spurs.'

Numbly, a dumb animal being led to the slaughter, Schulze followed her, while outside the world rocked and trembled, as if the Day of Judgement had come at last.

Nerves jingling and mind racing, von Dodenburg flung himself into the driving cab of the five-ton halftrack, while his troopers swarmed up on to the deck. He ran his eye along the instrument panel, said a quick prayer and turned the ignition key. At the same moment another salvo of mortar bombs straddled the castle. The halftrack shook, as shrapnel rattled off its steel sides like tropical rain on a tin roof. Von Dodenburg did not even notice. His whole being was concentrated on the halftrack's motor.

Nothing! Just a throaty growl.

He forced himself to count off thirty seconds exactly. He didn't want to flood the motor. Then he tried again, as, behind him on the deck, the troopers fumbled with their dreadful weapon, already dressed in *Ami* protective clothing and goggles. The throaty growl became a whining dirge. Von Dodenburg felt a sense of hope. 'Come on, you bitch,' he cursed.

More bombs hurtled out of the snow-heavy sky. Behind the halftrack, one of the onion towers disappeared in a ball of vicious red flame. Suddenly the halftrack gave a great jerk. The motor was starting! Thick black smoke started to pour from the exhaust. He hung on to the key and the whole vehicle shook and trembled like some metal monster trying to rouse itself from a deep sleep.

'Start!' he prayed, for every minute counted. 'Please God, *let it start*.' There was a thunderous roar and the motor burst into life. Von Dodenburg needed no second invitation. He pressed home the gear stick and let out the clutch. The halftrack jerked forward, rattling at every plate. The civilians, milling around in panic, scattered. Von Dodenburg felt the tracks crunch and bump over the dead, but he had no time to swerve and avoid them. They were dead anyway. It was now a question of trying to save the still living. He slammed home second gear. The halftrack began to gather speed. He swung out of the exit. Now, through the slit in the front armour, he could see the long line of *Amis* advancing through the snow, plodding forward with their rifles at the high port like weary farm labourers returning home after a hard day's labour in the fields. Soon they'd be moving faster than that, those of them who would survive the terrible thing that was now going to happen to them.

'But why the spurs?' Schulze protested, well aware that he was still standing there stark naked while the Countess knelt at his booted feet and fussed around with the silver spurs that had once belonged to her husband.

'If one is to ride successfully,' she answered thickly, not daring to look at that enormous piece of flesh dangling there and almost touching her dishevelled hair, 'one needs the right kind of spurs, big and – *sharp*!' She rolled the wheel, feeling the sharp spikes lovingly.

Schulze flung a wild look around the big bedroom, the bed situated in its centre on a raised dais, almost as if it were a throne. But there was no escape. He was trapped with this crazy woman and her shitting spurs!

Suddenly she looked up at him sharply, the massive piece of meat only millimetres away from her face. She drank in the sight, panting feverishly, unable to contain herself any longer. '*Sergeant, Schulze,*' she gasped as she fell forward on to the white carpet, '*I command you to ride me for Germany!*'

CHAPTER 6

Von Dodenburg pressed his foot hard down on the accelerator. The halftrack's speed increased as it rattled down the track, spewing a wake of flying snow behind it and getting rapidly closer to the line of brown-clad men. Behind him his young troopers crouched in tense expectation, hands holding their weapons, wet with sweat. On either side were dead Alsatians, caught in that initial mortar bombardment, bodies already stiffening in the freezing cold. They passed the little *Luftwaffe* pilot for whom time had run out. His upper body had been flayed by the shrapnel, the flesh ripped off the torso in chunks to expose the rib cage.

'No more frigging breakfasts in bed with field mattresses* for that frigging flyboy,' one of the troopers commented sourly, and spat at the corpse. '*His* flying days are over!'

Von Dodenburg, holding on to the bucking wheel, shook his head in mock wonder. How brutal his eighteen-year-olds had become in these last months! Could one ever let them loose in civilized society again? "Get the fuckers home first, Kuno,' that hard little voice at the back of his mind rasped harshly. 'Get them home!'

Von Dodenburg frowned. Of course, that was the only attitude to take. He had to get the survivors, brutalized as they were, back to the Reich. He flung home second gear. The metal monster shook at every rivet. The motor howled. In the back the troopers held on for their lives. Von Dodenburg swung the halftrack round in a flurry of whirling wild snow. For a moment the advancing Americans seemed unaware of what was happening, but already here and there some of them were reacting to the new danger. Slugs began to

* Nickname for officers' mistresses

cut the air and one of them was firing a light machine gun of some kind. Von Dodenburg could hear the bullets whining as they bounced off the halftrack's armour.

Holding the madly swaying vehicle, he yelled above the racket, 'Gunner prepare to fire! And for God's sake, don't miss!' The leather-clad trooper, face covered by a frightening mask of the same material, complete with goggles, nodded his head in understanding. He knew what the C.O. meant. In a moment the vehicle would stop so that he could fire accurately. But he would only have one chance, standing there upright behind the terrible weapon, a sitting duck once the *Amis* started firing at him. He tensed.

Von Dodenburg hesitated no longer. The leading Americans were less than sixty metres away. He said a quick prayer that the range was correct and that the young gunner wouldn't miss. He hit the brakes. The halftrack shuddered to a stop. Almost immediately the Americans began to fire. A burst of machine-gun fire ran the length of the vehicle like someone running a bar along a line of iron railings. Von Dodenburg ducked instinctively, as tracer bullets exploded across the steel windscreen, blinding him momentarily in brilliant incandescent, white light.

But the young trooper at his deadly gun didn't flinch. He pressed the trigger and there was a vicious hiss like some primeval monster drawing its first awesome breath, as a thick yellow rod of flame spurted from the gun. Out and up it curved whilst in front of it the snow shrivelled away to reveal the suddenly charred and steaming earth below.

Suddenly the flaming rod curved downwards. Burning particles of fuel oil splattered everywhere. The air was full of the stench of burning. Horrified, transfixed, face contorted, von Dodenburg watched the progress of that all-consuming lethal flame as it struck home.

It hit the leading Americans and they erupted into flame, at once becoming human torches. Wildly they scattered, the greedy flames consuming their flesh at a tremendous speed, charring it, shrivelling it, cracking it so that the blood-red gore oozed out of the black bubbling skin. Men went mad. Screaming like banshees they ran back and forth, flames pouring from their blackened bodies. Others tried to keep their heads. They threw themselves into the snow. Writhing back and forth, they tried to extinguish those all-consuming flames. To no avail! Their struggles, then, got fainter and fainter until finally they simply lay there like stranded fish, gasping ever more weakly and letting it happen.

A group of the Negro infantrymen ran for the cover of a depression and attempted to set up a machine gun. Von Dodenburg watching them, felt the bile mounting in his throat, his face contorted with the horror of it all. They hadn't a chance. He saw their frightened black faces under their too-big helmets and knew they would be dead within the next minute. 'Run for it,' he cried to himself. '*For Chrissake, run for it!*'

But even as he thought the words, the young trooper had spotted them and was swinging his weapon round in their direction, eyes behind the black goggles gleaming like those of a man demented. Again he fired. A great hiss, a sucking in of air, and once more that terrifying rod of flame shot out, scorching and searing everything in its path. It hit a grove of firs which ignited at once, falling like flaming matchsticks. Then, like a vicious yellow wild-cat, the flame curled itself round the hollow. In an instant, the snow melted away in a great hiss. But even that noise could not conceal the terrible screams of the soldiers. Von Dodenburg gasped. The negroes were staggering out like drunken men, limbs already aflame, moaning and shrieking, some of them already blinded and feeling their way with outstretched hands. Aghast, but unable to avert his gaze, von Dodenburg watched as they staggered towards the burning wood. Until at last he was able to vomit, his skinny body racked as if in mortal pain.

Two hundred yards away, Colonel Petersen blew three blasts on his whistle and cried in a voice that was broken and full of emotion, 'Pull back, boys. *For God's sake pull back!*'

The first attack of Colonel Petersen's Fighting Coons on Schloss Falkenstein had failed miserably.

The *Amis* were mortaring once again and every time a salvo thundered to the ground, the walls shook and the dust of centuries came drifting down from the high vaulted roof in a thin sad rain. 'All right, Corporal Matz,' von Dodenburg ordered, his voice dry and weary, as if he had run out of all emotion, 'report please.'

In a voice thickened with years of cheap cigars and even cheaper schnapps, Matz rasped, 'Not too bad, sir. We lost twenty men, with ten wounded, but they'll soldier on.'

Von Dodenburg nodded. So he had lost ten per cent of his effectives already. 'And the Alsatians?'

Matz looked at him, suddenly contemptuous. 'Should we bother, sir? Those piss pansies have had it. Couldn't fight their way outa paper bag now, that's my opinion.'

'Are they holding their share of the perimeter?'

Matz shrugged. 'Well, sir, they're in position, if that's what yer mean. But that's about all. Next time the *Amis* attack, the whole frigging bunch of them will pick up their hind legs and hoof it.'

There was a mumble of agreement from the others. This first taste of total war had turned the civilians into devout cowards. Now they were broken reeds. There was no relying on them any more.

Von Dodenburg absorbed the information and then asked, 'And what of the *Amis?*'

'Probing, sir. Niggers they might be, but they don't give up so easily. Ever since it got dark, they've been out there in twos and threes, trying to find weak spots in the perimeter.' He laughed hollowly, but there was no answering warmth in his bloodshot eyes. 'Frigging invisible men they are in the darkness. Got their own built-in camouflage. Get it?'

Nobody else laughed.

Von Dodenburg asked one final question of this 'Old Hare'

who had been with him since the great days of the victory in France back in 1940, in what now seemed another age. 'And the weather?'

'*Scheisskalt*, sir,' Matz growled. 'If yer'll forgive my frigging French? A real ball-cruncher. Gonna freeze hard this night, I'll be bound.' He looked a little contemptuously at the weary young faces of the 'greenbeaks', as he called them. 'Some of you wet-tails is gonna earn the Frozen Meat Order.'

Von Dodenburg sat back in the damp straw and considered. The snow had stopped and the frost had set in. That could well mean that the morrow would bring one of those typical early winter days in the High Vosges: brilliant blue skies with visibility that seemed to stretch to eternity. The best kind of flying weather possible. He knew that he had only one chance to save his battered regiment. They would have to make their breakout by dawn. The question was – *how?*

'Matz,' he asked after a few moments, while his men stared at him expectantly, like children who had implicit faith in the father's ability to solve all problems, 'have you any idea where there is a weak point in the *Ami* line?'

'Well, sir, my guess is that they moved in close under cover of darkness on all sides. And as you know, there's precious little cover on this hill. The only reason the buggers haven't been able to get right under the walls themselves is because of the minefields.' He sniffed and whipped off the dewdrop. 'If they was more experienced, they'd know that the snowfield is thick enough to allow them to cross the minefield without too much trouble. Just happens they ain't old hares like. . . .' He stopped short. He could see that the C.O. was no longer listening.

Von Dodenburg's mind raced. Of course, that was it! The *Amis* were playing it by the book. They had seen the skull-and-crossbone signs which marked the minefields and were steering clear of them, not realizing that the thick layer of snow would easily stand the normal two or three pound pressure necessary to detonate the deadly anti-personnel mines.

Matz looked at him and said tonelessly, 'Sir, if you're

thinking of taking Wotan out through that minefield, you ought to have another think.'

'What do you mean, Matz?' he asked sharply, suddenly angry with the little one-legged corporal.

'The snow's frozen stiff, sir. They'd hear us right off. And what would the shit-shovellers do, as soon as the alarm was raised?' He answered his own question. 'Why, they'd plaster the field with mortar bombs and you'd have them nasty little buggers going off all around. Legs, bollocks, feet'd be flying everywhere.' He grabbed the front of his stained and ragged trousers dramatically. 'I, for one, ain't gonna have my outside plumbing shot off by any black nigger. No sir! Corporal Matz has something of very great value, very great value indeed, hanging down here.'

'Go crap in yer hat!' a familiar voice boomed scornfully. 'With that little worm of yourn, you'd couldn't even make a frigging nun blink!'

The men spun round. Schulze stood there, leaning against the wall casually, helmet tipped to the back of his shaven skull, dressed in what appeared to be a pre-war officer's dress uniform, wearing, for some strange reason, spurs, their points tipped with red, as if they had been dipped in blood.

'Sergeant Schulze!' von Dodenburg breathed. 'I'd forgotten about you. Where in the devil's name have *you* been, you big rogue.'

Schulze slouched into a sloppy salute and said, 'Been looking for a uniform, as commanded, sir.' Then he added obscurely. 'I was detained. Forced to ride for Germany, so to speak.' He relaxed and his spurs jingled.

Matz's mouth dropped open. 'What d'yer frigging mean – *ride for Germany*?'

Schulze let his gaze drop modestly to his dirty hands, which seemed as scratched as his unshaven face. 'One has one's obligations, Corporal, you know, we of the aristocracy.' He took out a pair of red silk knickers, trimmed with expensive black lace, dabbing his scratches delicately. '*Noblesse oblige*, you know – *peasant!*'

Matz opened his mouth to make an angry retort, but von Dodenburg held up his hand for silence. 'Now Schulze, we haven't got times for playing games. What's the deal, eh?'

'It's the minefield, sir. I've got an idea, so they wouldn't be able to hear us passing through it.'

'Well, shoot!'

Hastily Schulze blurted out his idea. When he was finished he looked around at the circle of tense engrossed faces, almost as if he half expected a round of applause.

Matz, for his part, impressed as he was, was not going to allow his old comrade to indulge himself. Sourly he grunted, 'Might work. The *Amis* aren't too swift in the upper storey, especially them black apes o' theirn.'

Von Dodenburg rubbed his unshaven jaw, as he attempted to work out the details and the timing. Finally he made up his mind. 'Well, Schulze,' he conceded, 'you might well have a solution there. At the worst we *could* confuse the *Amis*. But there's a problem – Grafin von Falkenstein.'

Schulze laughed. 'I don't think you need worry about Gertrud any more, sir,' he said and, clicking his fingers, he called, '*Gerti!*'

The door swung open slowly, as they turned to look. For a moment nothing happened, then the Doberman lurched in, hiccupped and slid into a corner, where it crossed its legs like some tame poodle and fell into a deep sleep at once. '*Pissed!*' Schulze said. 'Didn't know dogs drank bubbly.'

Von Dodenburg stared at him and stuttered, 'And the Countess? What about the Countess?'

Schulze smiled and said, 'Here she is, sir. Come on, Gerti,' he urged. 'Move yer ass, willyer!'

'Christ on a crutch,' Matz breathed in awe, '*Gerti!*'

Grafin von Falkenstein swayed into the room, obliviously as drunk on 'bubbly', as her dog. She spotted Schulze and stretched out her naked arms drunkenly, the pungent reek of fertility emanating from her half-clad body. 'Why do you resist me, Schatzi?' she breathed, swaying alarmingly. 'I am yours, lover, whenever you command.' She giggled like a schoolgirl and tried to grab the front of Schulze's trousers, while the others stared at her spellbound and shocked into total silence by this transformation. Schulze, however, took it all in his stride – perhaps it was all part-and-parcel of his newly acquired '*noblesse oblige*'. He slapped her importuning fingers away from his flies and said firmly, 'Gerti, you just sit down there and be quiet and listen to what the officer has to say.'

Gerti nodded drunkenly and did just that, simpering. She was fast asleep and snoring lightly within five seconds flat.

CHAPTER 7

Colonel Petersen radiated strength and confidence. As he passed from foxhole to foxhole, he had a kind word, a slap on the back, a little joke or quip for each of his young black soldiers. 'We'll take 'em tomorrow, men, don't worry!' he repeated over and over again, as Wolf, muffled up to the eyes, followed in his wake, the cold slowly working its way up his legs so that he thought he might well lose control of his limbs and fall at any moment. 'The weather's fine and we're gonna have air support tomorrow. There'll be a hot meal, turkey, gravy, creamed potatoes and all the trimmings, I promise you, fellers.' And he would slap some bent-shouldered, frozen youth across his skinny shoulders as if he *really* believed his own promises.

Behind him Wolf's frown deepened. TAC Air definitely would support Petersen's Fighting Coons on the morrow. They really had promised this time, now that radio contact had been established once more. But as for the food, Wolf knew that was a pious hope. Those damned redneck drivers had obviously bugged out, taking the rations with them. The hungry riflemen would have to fight on the morrow with what they could find in their pockets and packs. Most of them would go into action against the damned castle without even a hot drink of coffee inside them and it would be at least another forty-eight hours before supplies could reach them from the plain below. If they didn't take the castle, Petersen's soldiers would die of exposure. Already they had about reached the limit of their endurance.

His rounds done, Petersen relaxed, as much as anyone could in that bitter freezing wind that seemed to come straight from Siberia. 'Well, Wolf,' he sighed, 'that's about it. I don't think I can do much more to put heart into the boys. God knows how they stand this cold.'

Wolf nodded and tried not to look at the charred 'things' higher up the castle slope which marked the furthest yesterday's abortive attack had reached. 'I've spent most of my life in New York State, sir,' he said, trying to stop his shivering, 'and there we have some winters! But I've never known cold like this. It strikes to the very marrow!'

'Yes, I know. They won't stand another day of this kind of weather, Wolf. I reckon that a good half of them have already got slight frostbite. If we don't get under cover soon, they'll be cutting the feet off them.' He frowned and cocked his head as the hammering up above them in the castle began once more. 'What do you think they're up to in that damned castle, hammering away like that?'

Wolf shrugged. 'I'm afraid I don't know, sir. It's pretty obvious they have no heavy weapons up there or they would have taken out those mortars of yours by now.' He paused and listened as the wind whistled across the frozen slope, bringing the sound of renewed hammering with it. 'Perhaps they're trying to repair that damned flame thrower after that second salvo hit it.'

Petersen's frown deepened. 'I don't think they'll dare try that one on us again. The mortar people up there on the slope have got orders to take it out with everything they've got, immediately it appears. No sir,' he growled. 'This time that flame thrower will turn out to be a death trap for the Krauts. All the same, Wolf, I'd dearly like to know what the Sam Hill game they're playing up there at this time of night.' Then he dismissed the matter with a curt, 'All right, Wolf, let's see if we can get a couple of hours of shut-eye before dawn. It's gonna be a long, long day.' He sighed wearily, suddenly feeling his age. Slowly the two officers started to wander back to their own foxhole. Above them the hammering continued.

Von Dodenburg's nerves were on edge. Try as he might, he could not stop the trembling of his hands, as that long icy night passed with leaden feet. He knew well that the renewed hammering would have alerted the *Amis* down below – he could just make out the tiny flickers of their fires in the forest – but could they guess what Wotan intended? That was the overwhelming question: 'God,' he cursed angrily, as he went up onto the battlements yet once again, 'it's triple-damned sick-making!'

He searched the terrain below for any sign of *Ami* activity, but there was none. The fires still flickered fitfully; the icy wind continued to race across the frozen snowfield. *Nothing!*

In spite of the freezing wind, von Dodenburg found himself sweating. He knew why. It was the tension. Dawn, another three hours away, might well mean the end of SS Assault Regiment Wotan. It took only one slip, once they were out there in the open – the minefield was absolutely bare of cover – and it would be a massacre. His weary troopers wouldn't stand a chance.

With an effort he pulled himself together, wiped the sweat from his forehead and controlled his breathing. He had to think this through clearly. With a bit of luck Schulze's dodge might work. The Alsatians whom they had selected to drive the metal monsters would be only too glad to keep on going until their gas ran out or they felt safe enough to make a run for it back to their native villages and go undercover, all thoughts of a German reconquest of Alsace conveniently forgotten. The local 'civvies', as Schulze called them contemptuously, had had a bellyful of 'military glory'; all they wanted to do now was to go home.

But what if the Ami *jabos arrived at dawn and caught them in the middle of the minefield?* The question sprang frighteningly into von Dodenburg's mind as he sheltered there on the battlements, the wind whipping his ragged uniform. What then? What could he do to prevent the slaughter that would occur? He bit his bottom lip until he felt the warm taste of his own blood, as he fought back the old sensation of panic which threatened to overwhelm him once again with the thought of the morrow. After an effort of willpower, he forced himself to think. With the two forces so close together, the *Amis* would use some kind of identification on the ground to ensure their pilots didn't bomb their own troops. But what type of identification would they employ? In the *Wehrmacht* in the old days, when there was equipment a-plenty and everything still went by the book, they had placed purple panels of bright cloth twenty metres in front of their own lines and then made an arrow with other panels to place behind them, indicating the direction of the enemy troops. But that had been in the old days.

In Russia they had learned to improvise. In those remote snowbound wastes, they had insufficient transport to carry such equipment around with them. Their positions had been indicated by stamping a huge swastika in the snow and then, when their own aircraft were spotted coming in for the attack, they had fired green flares to make sure that the flyboys recognized that these were German positions, followed by red flares streaming towards the Ivans' lines. That was until the Popovs had caught on to the Germans' tactics and had begun turning the tables, scrawling swastikas behind their own lines and firing red flares towards the German positions. Often, thereafter, the *Luftwaffe*, their pilots by then a bunch of half-trained eighteen-year-olds, had bombed their own troops! As the weary old hares of the Russian campaign had complained, without rancour, after such bombings, 'Even God on High is against us poor old stubble-hoppers. *Now he's shitting frigging Krupp steel onto our poor old grey heads*!'

Von Dodenburg pursed his blood-stained lips thoughtfully. If the *Ami jabos* did appear and their ground troops had to improvise as they had done in Russia, was there some way of turning the tables, tricking the US pilots into. . . . His train of thought was suddenly interrupted.

From down below came a lone voice, powerful yet plaintive, carried up to the ramparts by the wind. Von Dodenburg shivered. What did it mean? Why was anyone singing in the middle of the night in this God-forsaken place? Did that *Ami* – he guessed it had to be an American, a black one at that – realize that he might well die at dawn, far away from his own country, for a cause that wasn't his?

Von Dodenburg stood there listening to that lone man singing in the darkness; then he turned and began to make his way down the echoing stairs, shoulders bent as if in defeat.

A mile away Master-Sergeant Lee heard it too and felt a renewal of hope. All that day he had been staggering in and out of those fir forests, up and down the snowbound hills, desperately hoping that he would find the battalion on the other side. More than once he had been tempted to give up, to lie down and give into Nature, drifting into a sleep from which he would never awake. But he had fought off the temptation, telling himself firmly that the battalion needed him for the final showdown with the SS. 'Gotta keep them black butts moving,' he had whispered to himself, as he slogged forward through the knee-deep snow. 'Keep on movin', guys – for the honour of the Regiment,' and his eyes had glittered crazily, as he forced himself to continue his lone struggle against the bitter elements.

By now his toes were frost-bitten, as well as the tips of his fingers which felt like clumsy, awkward sausages. His uniform was soaked and frozen in patches. Icicles hung from his nostrils and his eyebrows glistened white with hoar frost, so that he thought that he must look like his own grandpappy.

Now he heard the song, so faint that he could only guess that it was one of those old Southern spirituals with which his boys comforted themselves when times were bad. He staggered to a stop and stood there, swaying in the moonlight, drinking in the song. For a moment the tough Sergeant felt as if he would cry at the poignant beauty. The unknown singer was pouring his whole heart into it – his loneliness, his bitterness at a Motherland which rejected him because his skin was black, his desire to love and be loved.

Master-Sergeant Lee swallowed and licked his cracked lips. 'I'm coming, Colonel,' he croaked. 'I'm coming, sir. Don't start nothin' without me, sir.' He staggered on.

CHAPTER 8

To the east the horizon was beginning to flush a blood-red. Already the black shadows were sweeping across the hills like silent hawks flying westwards. The snowfield began to glitter and sparkle once more and everything started to stand out in harsh black relief – the shattered turrets of Schloss Falkenstein, the body-littered slope, the foxhole line of the Americans dug in below.

Von Dodenburg lowered his glasses. The *Amis* were apparently not aware of what they planned this morning. Here and there a thin trickle of grey smoke rose from their lines, where someone was obviously cooking on a fire of twigs and frozen leaves, but there were no signs of an imminent attack. The *Amis* obviously kept gentlemen's hours; they wouldn't attack before nine o'clock. To the east the dawn sky was clear. It was going to be a perfect winter's day, and that could mean only one thing. *The* Amis *would whistle up their dive-bombers!*

He dismissed the unpleasant thought. He would face up to that problem when it arose. He tucked the glasses into their case and said, 'Well, Matz, everything all right?'

Matz whipped yet another dewdrop from his bright red nose and answered, 'Everything in butter, sir. The boys are in position and the civvies are – well. . . .' He shrugged and didn't finish.

'Are the Alsatians getting cold feet?' von Dodenburg asked.

'No sir,' Matz sneered. 'Them yokels have heads full of puddin'. They ain't got that kind of imagination! No, what worries me, is that the shiteheels might fuck up the breakout. It takes only one of them to stall his engine and then the clock'll be really in the pisspot!'

Von Dodenburg smiled in spite of his anxiety. 'What a command of the German language you have, Corporal Matz! You could well be the Goethe of the 20th century.'

'Goethe?' Matz looked up at him suspiciously. 'Was he the feller what wrote them dirty books?' he asked.

Von Dodenburg dismissed the question. 'Where's Sergeant Schulze?' he demanded and began to walk to the stairs.

Matz flipped a wad of hardened dirt from under his fingernail with his bayonet and held it out at an exaggerated angle, as if he were some society woman daintly lifting a cup. 'Senior Sergeant Schulze,' he said in an affected accent, 'don't consort with the likes of me any more, sir. He's taking morning coffee with the aristocracy, and no doubt trying to cock his big leg. . . .' He was interrupted by an all-too-familiar voice as it boomed: 'None of that dirty talk in front of the C.O., Corporal Matz. And remember that you are talking about my bride-to-be, *Arse-with-Ears*!' Schulze, washed and shaved and obviously well pleased with himself, threw von Dodenburg a tremendous salute and added, 'Of course, that's when my lawyers work out the details of the dowry naturally.'

Von Dodenburg shook his head in bewilderment. 'Bride to be . . . lawyers . . . details of the dowry,' he muttered to himself, as if he could not quite believe his own ears.

Schulze beamed at him. 'Once our beloved Führer, Adolf Hitler, has achieved final victory,' he boomed, 'the Countess and I will probably retire to her ancestral estates in East Prussia. She has grown rather weary of Froggieland. There, of course, we will ensure that the Falkenstein-Schulze line continues. We're both very hot on the lineage, you see.'

Matz moaned and clapped his hand to his head, while for his part, von Dodenburg looked at Schulze with icy disapproval.

Schulze got the message. 'I've kitted the Countess out, sir. Uniform and gear from one of the dead troopers. She'll be going with us in the Second Platoon,' he snapped, military and business-like now. 'I'm putting Corporal Matz in charge of it.'

Von Dodenburg nodded, conceding defeat. 'All right, Sergeant Schulze, let's go and have a look at the men.'

The survivors of SS Wotan were lined up in the courtyard, stamping their feet on the frozen cobbles, here and there smoking a last precious cigarette: some of the more nervous urinating for the umpteenth time against the grey walls.

Sergeant Schulze 'built his ape', as the old hares called it. Feet spread, huge hands clasped to his hips, enormous chest puffed out, he bellowed, 'All right, you bunch of poxed-up penguins, officer on parade! SS Assault Regiment Wotan – *attention!*'

As one, a hundred and fifty pairs of feet snapped to attention. In an instant all weariness, fear or slackness had vanished. Now they stood rigidly upright, eyes fixed on some distant object, faces proud and determined. Schulze swung round and threw von Dodenburg a tremendous salute. 'SS Assault Regiment Wotan, *all present and correct, sir!*' he barked.

Von Dodenburg gazed at their hard young faces, pleased with what he saw. Despite the privations and the hardships of these last months, there was no sign of weakness in their faces. He knew instinctively that, if called upon to do so, they would fight to the bitter end. But it wouldn't come to that, he told himself; he was going to get them safely back to the Reich. Over these last years he had led far too many young men to their deaths; these would live.

'Stand easy!' he shouted. Their right feet shot out and they relaxed a little.

He wasted no more time. Already the winter sun was beginning to creep over the snow-tipped peaks. 'Soldiers, comrades,' he cried over the harsh cawing of the rooks and the first low rumble of an obstinate engine. 'This morning we go into action once more. I make no appeals to your love of the Fatherland, the honour of SS Wotan or anything of that nature. Instead I ask you to bear this in mind. All that is needed is one final effort on your part. If we must fight, then we will.' He paused. 'But I hope that we will trick the enemy and vanish before he knows we have gone. So it is imperative that there should be no stragglers to give away the rest.'

At his side, Schulze slapped the butt of the machine pistol

draped across his massive chest significantly and glowered at the men, as if daring them even to think of such things.

'Soldiers,' von Dodenburg raised his voice so those in the rear rank could hear his every word, 'we march *not to fight but to freedom.*'

In the courtyard the first engine thundered into ear-splitting life, sending the rooks flying high. Von Dodenburg jerked his clenched fist up and down three times, the infantry signal for advance. Schulze bellowed over the roar of a second motor, 'All right, you heard the C.O.! Come on, you dogs. *Do you want to live for ever?*'

Half a kilometre away Colonel Petersen, followed by Captain Wolf, was also inspecting his men as they began to form up in their skirmish lines, faces frozen but determined. Time and again, Petersen nodded his approval as one of his young black soldiers smiled at him and called, 'Morning, Colonel, suh!'

'They'll do it this time, Wolf,' he repeated. 'The men'll do it.'

'Air is expected at zero nine hundred hours, sir,' Wolf reminded him as they had reached the end of the first skirmish line, the men already taking off their gloves so that they could fire their weapons more effectively. Here and there NCOs were shouting, 'All right, you guys, off with them packs!' Others were walking along the line handing out grenades, which were snatched eagerly by the men as if the deadly, little eggs were very precious.

Petersen nodded, noting that everything was going to plan. 'Thanks, Wolf. But do you think those flyboys will recognize our people?'

'I wouldn't trust them, sir,' Wolf advised. 'The flyboys are not very particular who they bomb. In Italy we used to call TAC Air the American *Luftwaffe*, they bombed us so often. When they make their appearance, we'd better make it pretty clear where the start line of our attack is.'

'But the identification panels are with those damned traitors in the Weasels.'

'Yes, I know, sir.' Wolf tugged the bell-shaped pistol from his belt. 'Signal pistol, sir. A green flare over our own lines, a red one towards the enemy. That's the usual deal we use in the US Seventh Army.'

'Good.' Petersen accepted the pistol and the cartridges. 'I'll take over that job myself. I'm not gonna have any mistakes made now. We've pussy-footed around too long as it is. This morning we're killing Krauts, the whole durn shoot of them!' He glanced at his wrist-watch. 'Zero eight hundred hours. One to go,' he announced. 'By zero ten hundred, Captain, I want that castle captured and the enemy routed once and for all. This time Petersen's Fighting Coons are going to win.'

'*Los!*' von Dodenburg cried above the roar of the Sherman's 400 HP engine, and slapped its metal side enthusiastically, as if it were a race horse. The Alsatian driver needed no urging. He slipped home the massive gear. A whirl of track, burst of speed, and the big thirty-ton tank leading the convoy rumbled forward, swinging left and out into the open. One by one the other armoured vehicles, all of them packed with hopeful, frightened civilians, followed, heading for the downwards slope.

Von Dodenburg, followed by Sergeant Schulze, doubled to where his men were crouched in the shelter of the woods at the side of Schloss Falkenstein. 'Wheel 'em off, Corporal Matz,' he cried as he ran, 'wheel 'em off!'

'All right, piss pansies, don't just stand waiting for the wet fart to hit the side of the thundermug – *move!*'

They moved, with von Dodenburg and Schulze bringing up the rear, both of them tense and expectant, waiting for the inevitable American reaction.

From the hill on the other side of the valley there came the thick crump of explosives – three quick grunts in succession.

Three trails of white smoke hurtled into the sky. And an eerie, unnatural keening that made von Dodenburg want to grind his teeth. Then the first bomb hit the leading Sherman. It reeled as if struck by a sudden tornado, but when the smoke had cleared the tank still rumbled on, a bright silver scar gouged in its turret. The second bomb exploded harmlessly in the snow. The third was a direct hit. The second halftrack, crowded with men, came to an abrupt stop with a dreadful crash. For a moment nothing happened. Then the vehicle's petrol tank exploded. Like a gigantic blow torch the flame seared the men in the back. Screaming and shrieking, bodies alight in a flash, they fell over the sides, posturing wildly as they tried in vain to slap out the flames, like members of some crazed, lascivious dance.

'Poor shits,' Schulze muttered as he clambered over the rusty barbed wire which marked the extent of the minefield. 'Didn't even know what hit 'em.'

Von Dodenburg nodded, as a fresh wave of burning petrol swept over the burning men, and concentrated on the task at hand.

'*Don't panic, men!*' Colonel Petersen yelled as the metal monsters broke out of the column, scattering wildly as the mortarmen brought down a furious barrage. 'We've got 'em by the nuts!'

Wolf, who had not fired a shot in anger since the US Army had landed in North Africa back in '42 (and then it had been at a Frenchman, and he had missed) clutched the long steel of the bazooka uncertainly. In front of him the battered Sherman weaved back and forth all over the place, throwing up a huge wake of snow, as if the driver was drunk or mad, or perhaps both. He certainly was offering a tempting target, even for a devout coward like Wolf.

'All right, Wolf,' Petersen said, as everywhere his skirmish line began to fire at the advancing vehicles, 'you're in range. Take the bastard out!'

Wolf sent a quick prayer winging heavenwards. Now the Sherman seemed to fill the whole horizon. He took aim. His finger curled round the trigger. He pressed it and closed his eyes to blot out the monster hurtling towards them, intent on crushing them to a red pulp. The tube shivered violently on his shoulder. He felt a flash of heat at the side of his face. He opened his eyes. The rocket was shrieking towards the Sherman, trailing fiery red sparks behind it. A sudden hollow boom, metal striking metal. The Sherman shuddered to a halt. For what seemed an age to the mesmerized Wolf, nothing seemed to happen. Then the Sherman fell apart! A tremendous explosion racked it. Great shards of metal flew everywhere. The ten-ton turret whirled through the air like a child's toy. A head rolled towards Wolf and trundled to a stop. It stared at him, pipe still clasped between the teeth. Wolf retched violently, then he was sick.

What happened next was not war, it was a massacre. Completely unnerved by the destruction of the halftrack and the Sherman, the panic-stricken Alsatians started to abandon their vehicles, throwing up their arms and screaming for mercy. But the black soldiers' blood was up. They poured a hail of fire into the civilians who went down in a screaming confused heap of flailing arms and legs.

A driver panicked at the sight and tried to reverse. In his haste, he overlooked the other halftrack behind him and they crashed together with a great metallic boom. The engine of the second halftrack was ruptured by the impact and the fuel flooded out immediately. In a flash it was alight and burning fiercely, engulfing both the vehicles now locked together in an embrace of death. Men were scattered everywhere beating the flames, trying to escape. But there was no escape. One by one they succumbed, collapsing in the blackened snow.

One of the halftrack's ammunition lockers exploded in the heat and tracer zig-zagged crazily into the sky. A civilian, running frantically to escape the racing flames, staggered, flung up his arms and clawed the air as if he were scuttling up the rungs of an invisible ladder. He flopped to the ground. Next instant the flames had swept over him, leaving behind a shrivelled piece of charred flesh.

'*Bello*!' Grafin von Falkenstein cried, as Wotan advanced in single-file across the snow-covered surface of the minefield. But already the black hound, crazed by the screams, the flames, and the mad noise coming from the opposite slope, had broken away and was racing at a tremendous pace over the snowfield.

'Stop that dog!' von Dodenburg yelled. 'Stop . . .'

His command was drowned by the crackle of Matz's Schmeisser. Slugs stitched snow all around the fleeing dog's feet, but Bello seemed to bear a charmed life. Racing all out, tongue dangling from the side of its mouth, it headed straight for the *Ami* positions.

Schulze raised his Schmeisser and fired, but Bello's luck held out and a moment later he had vanished over the slope, barking crazily, as if he had deliberately gone out of his way to betray them to the *Amis*.

Matz swung round, face furious. 'You and yer fucking aristocrats, Schulze!' he cried. 'Now see what's happened? Yer can't even trust their fucking aristocratic hounds!'

Schulze opened his mouth, but von Dodenburg jammed his elbow into the NCO's ribs. 'Knock it off,' he growled. 'Save your breath. Let's not waste any more time. That damned dog is going to give us away. At the double, men! Come on; let's get to the cover of the woods. Only half a kilometre away, boys!' But, as he said the words, he knew they might as well have been half a million kilometres off. They'd never make it now. They broke into a shambling run.

As the great black hound, trailing its silver chain behind it, came hurtling across the snow towards them, eyes wild with terror, Colonel Petersen realized immediately what was going on. It explained exactly why the Krauts had used their armour so inexpertly, allowing the armour to be wasted so easily by a bunch of lightly armed infantrymen. The armour had been a feint. The bulk of the SS were escaping on foot, just over the damned hill, and they were doing so *over the minefield*! His weary face lit up. He'd got them at last, by the short and curlies.

Frantically waving his hands, ignoring the exploding ammunition from the burning armour and the panic-stricken Alsatians running for cover, he yelled 'Cease fire. . . . For God's sake, cease fire!'

The firing stopped and the silence was broken only by the crackle of flames and the moans of the wounded. 'Listen fellers, we're slaughtering the wrong steer!' he yelled. Colonel Petersen pointed to the hilltop. 'They're over there, men. The Kraut SS are over there, out in the open, trying to make a run for it. And are we gonna let them get away with it?'

The answer came back in one great roar! '*No suh. We ain't about to, Colonel suh!*'

'Then what in tarnation are we waiting for?' Colonel Petersen drew his pistol and waved it above his head like some 19th century cavalry leader flourishing his sword. 'Follow me, men!'

They ran forward up the slope, knee-deep in the snow, bayonets glinting in the thin rays of the sun. Colonel Petersen slipped and went down to his knees. But he was up again in a flash and struggling on, the clumsy-looking flare pistol lying where he had fallen, unnoticed.

Behind them a suddenly deflated Wolf stared down at the big black hound which had appeared so surprisingly from nowhere, and which was now crouched there exhausted, licking his boot hopefully. He patted it and whispered, 'Christ, let them do it *this time*!'

*

Two miles away Colonel 'Buzz' Hawkins, at twenty-three the youngest 'Bird Colonel' in the whole of the United States Army Air Corps, pressed his throat mike and rasped, 'Tiger Leader here . . . Tiger Leader here . . . Do you read me?'

To left and right his wingmen, flying in close with their Thunderbolts, raised gloved thumbs in acknowledgement. Buzz thrust his battered cap with its tarnished insignia further back on his crew-cut head and barked. ''Kay, now get this, you jerks. When I give the signal to attack, I want you in – *and out* – at double quick time. Got it?' 'Roger. . . . Roger.' The replies came back from his pilots, faces grinning back at him through the glittering mica of their cockpits.

'D'ya want to know why, guys?' Buzz continued with a lazy grin, though his eyes remained those of a born killer. 'I'll tell ya. Because I've got a date with a very hot frog body at zero twelve hundred hours this day, *exactement*. And I don't want you jerk-offs frigging up my love life. So haul ass, when I say so. Over and out.'

'Wilco. . . . wilco,' the replies came crackling in over the radio. It was typical Buzz. If he wasn't screwing, he was fighting. Didn't Buzz have the reputation of being the greatest cocksman in the whole of the E.T.O.?* What was it he always boasted in the officers' club when he had downed his customary half-dozen potent seventy-fives** before he went out to chase tail? *The guy who won't fuck, won't fight!*

Colonel 'Buzz' Hawkins had certainly proved that he could do both in his brief but meteoric career in the Air Corps. Now, as that bright silver V of dive-bombers flew ever closer to their target, his bold young pilots prepared to carry out the slaughter of the 'ground jobs' and hurry back to base to implement the second part of the C.O.'s motto.

Sergeant Lee sat down in the snow with a grateful sigh. But,

* European Theater of Operations
** A wartime American cocktail

in spite of his bruises, his frostbite, his overwhelming fatigue, he was happy at last. There they were – Petersen's Fighting Coons – advancing steadily up the snowbound hillside, bayonets glistening in the sun, breath fogging in the icy air, but even at this distance, radiating determination and confidence.

In front the C.O. marched on, occasionally waving his pistol at his men and shouting what Lee took to be encouragement at them, though he couldn't hear the words. By God, he told himself, they made a brave sight that stirred even his weary heart as they advanced on the enemy.

To Lee, it was as if he were watching a silent newsreel, the long brown skirmish line plodding up the slope, with beyond the unsuspecting enemy crawling slowly through the minefield, as yet unaware of the danger. But in this newsreel some of the participants were men he knew and loved, men with whom he had sweated and strained in the blinding heat of Georgia on training exercises, men with whom he had suffered the insults and indignities of the southern rednecks, men of his own race who were now standing tall and proving themselves to be one hundred per cent true Americans, as good as their white brothers. 'Go to it, guys!' he cried enthusiastically, waving his fist in the air. 'Give 'em hell!'

Von Dodenburg reacted immediately, as the first mortar bomb exploded in the minefield with a great roar, followed an instant later by a series of other explosions, turning everything in a flash into chaos, noise and horror. 'Stand fast!' he bellowed above the roar, as mine after mine exploded all around. 'For God's sake, *stand fast!*'

Schulze ripped off a quick burst and yelled out, 'You heard the C.O. *Stand frigging fast!*'

The old iron discipline of the Waffen SS gripped them once more. The troopers stopped where they were as another batch of mines detonated, flinging up a huge shower of earth and snow, showering their helmets with pebbles. Even the wounded, sprawled out on the smoking ground, stopped their piteous moaning.

Von Dodenburg swallowed hard. The game was up. The *Amis* had spotted them. Their infantry would be attacking soon, but they wouldn't dare enter the minefield, he knew that. So, they had minutes – perhaps five at the most – left. 'Smoke,' he yelled desperately. 'Every man who has a smoke grenade pull out the pin!'

Schulze winked at the Countess, who in her helmet and camouflaged overalls looked just another trooper. 'Keep it nice and hot for papa,' he whispered and pulled out his smoke grenade, in the same instant that another salvo of mortar bombs dropped to their front. The earth quaked and shivered beneath their feet, as if it were alive. Great moleholes appeared. Von Dodenburg cried above the thunderous roar, as his pale face was lashed by the blast, 'Grenade-throwers to the front. Pick up the wounded, the rest of you. We're going to advance under a smoke screen!' To make his order clear, he flung his own grenade towards his front where it exploded and a moment later thick white smoke began to billow upwards.

As the grenade-throwers formed up around him, he waved his arm and they marched forward, trying not to think of the instant death that lurked now beneath their feet; it took only one mortar bomb exploding in the right spot to start a lethal chain reaction which could decimate a whole platoon in an instant.

So they advanced, lobbing the grenades twenty to thirty metres to their front and rushing into the cover of the billowing white smoke, hoping that this would put the gunners on the hill opposite off; knowing, however, that once the smoke vanished the *Ami* mortars would find them again.

Then, as abruptly as it had started, the tremendous barrage ceased. One moment all was a hellish roar, the next the terrifying howl from the skies had stopped and they were stumbling forward through the smoke, the only sound their own harsh forced breathing.

Von Dodenburg guessed at once what was happening. They were too close to the *Amis* for their mortar men to take any more chances; they might well hit their own people. He stopped and gasped, 'No more bombs. No more smoke grenades!'

Everyone looked at von Dodenburg as the smoke began to drift away. What was going on in his mind? Why had they stopped? What in the devil's name was happening.

Schulze opened his mouth to speak but von Dodenburg stopped him with a hard look and said quite calmly, as if it was the most obvious thing in the world, 'Sergeant, order the men to fix bayonets.'

'Fix bayonets?' Schulze began incredulously. 'We of Wotan haven't fixed bayonets since . . .' He stopped short. Through a gap in the smoke he caught a glimpse of what was waiting for them. Lined along the rusty barbed-wire fence with its skull-and-crossbone warning signs, there were scores – hundreds – of black-faced men staring at them like spectators at some football game waiting for play to start.

In a dream, and hardly recognizing his own voice, Schulze commanded, 'SS Assault Regiment Wotan will fix bayonets – *FIX*!' There was a slither of blades being drawn from their sheaths, a click of steel as they were attached, the harsh slap of rifle butts being slammed against horny palms. Schulze, without turning, his eyes fixed hypnotically on the waiting blacks, their young faces wary yet resolute, as they, too, prepared to charge, followed the course of the drill movement. Then he snapped, voice still not quite under control, 'SS Assault Regiment Wotan ready to attack, *sir*!'

Von Dodenburg acknowledged the report with a casual salute, his gaze also fixed on the *Amis*. Wotan was hopelessly outnumbered; they hadn't a chance. This was the end of the road. He had failed after all. But he simply couldn't surrender. *He couldn't*!

He tugged out his pistol and clicked off safety, placing himself at the centre of the line. Behind him the walking wounded shuffled to take up their places. Von Dodenburg's eyes flooded with tears for an instant. What good men they were! Even his wounded were not prepared to abandon Wotan, now that they had lost. He raised his voice. 'SS Assault Regiment Wotan,' he called, breath fogging on the cold air, 'will prepare to advance!'

Behind the wire the negroes fumbled with their weapons, bayonets glinting in the sun's weak rays. 'Prepare to stand off an attack,' Colonel Petersen, standing bolt upright and unafraid, called. 'And good luck, boys!'

'Good luck to you, Colonel suh!' the hoarse cry ran along the line. Von Dodenburg noted the resolution in the Americans' voices, but he paid no attention to it. Nothing mattered now, save that Wotan went down fighting. He swallowed, raised his pistol and commanded, '*ADVANCE*!'

Slowly, their bayoneted rifles held across their skinny chests, the handful of ragged survivors, the wounded keeping up with their comrades the best they could, began to stumble forward towards the waiting Americans, each man wrapped in a cocoon of his own thoughts. SS Assault Regiment Wotan was going into its last attack.

Jo was different from the girls back home in the States. She didn't shave – she was hairy all over – and Buzz suspected she didn't wash too often either; but then she used a lot of perfume to cover the smell. But was she something in the hay! Like an animal. She couldn't seem to get enough of him. Only the other night, she'd taken his dong and. . . . suddenly Colonel 'Buzz' Hawkins forgot the delightful French whore and her charms. Down below, stark black against the blinding white field of snow, there were two groups of tiny figures advancing on each other. It was them! 'Tiger Leader to all,' he snapped through the throat mike. 'Do you see them?'

'Roger, Tiger Leader, affirmative.' The excited replies of his pilots crackled over the air waves.

Buzz assessed the situation, taking in the risks, calculating the best method of attack. They seemed to be armed only with hand guns. No flak. The sun was just above the horizon – no use to them. And, as usual, the *Luftwaffe* was absent. As the RAF types said, it was going to be 'a piece of cake'.

'Listen you guys,' he barked, forgetting radio procedure in the heady excitement of combat. 'We're gonna do it cab-rack style. I'll lead. But don't crowd me, guys. And anyone who overshoots this one buys a case of champagne in the club. Got it?'

'But Buzz,' someone protested over the radio, 'there's supposed to be some of our own joes down there. *Which is which?*'

The young Colonel screwed up his eyes against the glare of the sun on the snowfield. He could see no recognition panels, no kind of identification whatsoever. But he knew his ground jobs of old. They'd show some ID at the last moment, and then they beefed because they were occasionally shot up. Typical wooden-headed infantry.

'Don't cream yer drawers, Elmer,' he answered. 'Once we come in for the attack, they'll identify themselves *toot-damned-sweet!* Kay, here we go, boys. *Let's dance!*' He pushed forward the throttle and the fighter-bomber seemed to fall out of the sky.

'*Colonel!*' Wolf cried, as the first of the deadly silver birds roared down, while the rest hovered above the lone plane waiting for their turn, 'the pistol – *fire the flare pistol!*' At his feet Bello hid his head between his front paws in apprehension. Colonel Petersen did not hear Wolf's desperate shout, but he did hear the vicious snarl of the diving plane's engine. He paused and, with his free hand, felt for the signal pistol. His face blanched. *It wasn't there! He must have dropped it!* 'Oh, my God!' he breathed as, behind him, the line of advancing infantrymen faltered and came to a ragged halt, the roar of the plane's engine growing louder by the instant.

Colonel Petersen panicked. He turned to face his soldiers,

his eyes taking in that silver bird dropping from the sky as if it were intent on hurtling to destruction below. '*Scatter, men. In, God's name scatter!*'

One hundred metres away *Obersturmbannführer* von Dodenburg, the veteran, reacted with lightning speed and totally correctly. He pulled out his own flare pistol, crying as he did so, 'Hit the dirt. *Hit the dirt, men!*' Next moment the first green flare was sailing into the sky, followed an instant later by a red flare which burst over Petersen's confused men, colouring their upturned black faces an unnatural rosy hue.

Colonel Petersen raised his fists to the sky like a man accursed, despairing the cruelty of his fate, his face contorted as if pleading with God himself at the bitter injustice that was being done to him and his black soldiers. The first burst of machine gun fire shattered his glasses. Blinded, he staggered a few paces, then fell to his knees, head bent in the classic pose of supplication. '*NO!*' he screamed. '*NO!*' His scream of final protest seemed to go on for ever and ever.

Watching the awesome spectacle unfold with an air of finality, knowing that nothing could be done now, Captain Wolf felt the small hairs at the back of his head stand erect with fear. At his feet Bello whimpered miserably, and crouched expectantly for what must come.

'*NO!*' The dying Colonel shrieked one final despairing protest. Suddenly he fell, face forward into the snow, dead. Captain Wolf began to cry. The slaughter of Colonel 'Black Jack' Petersen's Fighting Coons had started.

Envoi

'What passing bells for those who died as cattle?
Only the monstrous anger of the guns.'

Wilfred Owen

'SS Assault Regiment Wotan!' Kuno von Dodenburg barked, the whirling snowstorm growing in fury by the instant, as he stood in the cobbled farmyard, the guns of the permanent barrage rumbling menacingly in the far distance, '*Das Regiment – STILLGESTANDEN!*'

As the survivors snapped to attention, the band of the *Leibstandarte* broke into the march *Preussens Gloria*, all blaring brass and the steady bombastic thumping of the big drum, while the immensely tall drum-major, ramrod-straight, jerked his baton up and down woodenly. In the slow, arrogant fashion of the SS, Kuno von Dodenburg raised his gloved hand to his battered cap and waited.

At the door of the farmhouse headquarters, Adolf Hitler, dwarfed by a great ankle-length black cloak, Blondi cowering at his heels, faltered when he saw the soldiers drawn up for inspection. His sallow face grew paler. They were nothing better than a pathetic handful of human wrecks standing there in the softly falling snow.

Shocked, he looked around his entourage (which now included a sulky looking blonde in the pre-war black uniform of an SS major) for enlightenment. Jodl shrugged slightly and looked away. The Führer must learn the truth for himself; these were the soldiers with whom he was going to fight his vaunted new counter-offensive. Keitel stared woodenly at some distant object known only to himself. Colonel-General Sepp Dietrich, the commander of the Sixth SS Panzer Army which would lead the assault, stepped forward and asked in his thick Bavarian accent, 'Would the Führer do me the honour of inspecting the troops?'

Bewildered and shaky, Hitler allowed himself to be escorted by two gigantic SS adjutants to where von Dodenburg stood, the snowflakes already caking his shoulders.

Obediently the entourage followed, the sulky blonde SS Major slapping her gleaming jackboots with an evil-looking whip as she did so, the expression on her face indicating that she would dearly love to use it, if she dare.

Standing just behind von Dodenburg, Sergeant Schulze swallowed hard as he recognized her. Would he be allowed to 'ride for Germany' again in such a delightful manner, he wondered suddenly, before Wotan was sent back to the front again.

Hitler, his rheumy eyes full of tears, took von Dodenburg's hand in both his like an affectionate sentimental old aunt. 'My dear von Dodenburg,' he quavered, lips trembling, 'what suffering you and your brave fellows have undergone since Cassino! A regiment of three thousand strong reduced to this . . .' Words failed him and he gestured weakly at the hundred-odd men who had survived the long march back to the Reich. 'But you have kept faith, *mein Lieber*. I shall always remember that. You have kept faith.' Momentarily Hitler's voice broke.

'*Jawohl, mein Führer*,' von Dodenburg snapped dutifully. Once, back in the great days of victory, those eyes of Hitler had been so full of fanatical magnetism that he had been forced to shiver whenever he looked into them. Now they seemed worn, drained, burned-out. They were the eyes of an old, old man. They meant nothing to him any more.

'I will inspect the parade,' Hitler said at last, as the two gigantic SS officers took his shaking arms to guide him up and down the pitifully thin ranks of SS Wotan.

Smartly von Dodenburg stepped to his side as the snowstorm increased its fury, as if some God on high was angered by this spectacle and meant to blot it out. Away at the front the guns continued their relentless bombardment, preparing for what was soon to come.

Feebly, Hitler let himself be guided up and down the ranks, pausing here and there to pat the wan face of one of von Dodenburg's eighteen-year-olds like a genial old uncle, exchanging a few words with one of the surviving 'old hares'.

But the men, even the young fanatics of the Hitler Youth, were not impressed, von Dodenburg could see that. Just like their leader, the men of SS Wotan were burnt-out cases. This bitter war had gone on too long. It was time to put an end to the conflict, they all knew that, before the enemy overran what was left of their poor homeland.

At the rear of the entourage Grafin von Falkenstein came level with Sergeant Schulze, towering above her like a white giant. Schulze winked knowingly and whispered out of the side of his mouth, 'I've still got the spurs, Gerti!'

She looked at him coldly, as if she had never seen him in her life before. Haughtily she slapped her boot with her whip and snapped, the complete Prussian aristocrat now, 'If it is of interest to you, Sergeant-whatever-your-name-is, I no longer ride. When our beloved Germany is in mortal danger, there is no time for self-indulgence.' She tapped her rakishly tilted cap with her whip, as if in some kind of parting salute, and passed on.

In the front rank just behind Schulze, Matz, rapidly vanishing in the driving snow, sniggered and whispered the words of the bawdy old soldiers' song, 'And the mate at the wheel had a bloody good feel at the girl I left behind me, eh mate? What price *lineage* now, Schulzi?'

Schulze went purple beneath his hood of snow. 'By the great whore of Buxtehude,' he stuttered out of the side of his mouth, 'where the dogs piss out of their ears, I'll have you for that Matzi. I'll frigging well have you.'

But Schulze would not be having his old running mate this December; before it was over Matz would be dead on the battlefield and he, himself, would be a hunted man with every man's hand against him.

Finally Hitler was finished with his inspection. Wearily, steps faltering in the ankle-deep snow, he returned to the cover of the farmhouse door.

Dietrich nodded to Kuno von Dodenburg. The young Colonel spun round and faced his men. 'SS Assault Regiment!' he commanded, as the military band struck up the *Badenweiler*,

Hitler's favourite march, 'will advance. *PARADE MARCH*!'

Skinny chests stuck out, hands pressed rigidly to their sides, they stamped by their Führer in the goose-step and then they were gone, disappearing into the snow like grey, defeated ghosts, mocked by that bold brassy music, full of martial pomp. Now, like Colonel 'Black Jack' Petersen's long-dead 'Fighting Coons', the men of SS Wotan were marching away for their date with destiny. This time they would not return. And at the front the cannon rumbled in anticipation.